"You should go out more. With me,"

Frank said teasingly.

Donna felt her mouth going dry. He was so close to her. She tried to remember the promises she'd made to herself. "I don't want you to get the wrong idea—"

Lightly he combed his fingers through her hair and brushed it away from her cheek. "I don't have any ideas at all yet, but I'm working on them."

Excitement, sudden and charged, filled him the way it never had before. This was something special, he thought. *She* was something special.

Donna had to struggle to keep her eyes from fluttering shut. With flagging determination, she shifted as far away as she could on the love seat. It amounted to an inch at best. Not nearly enough room to protect her from her emotions....

Dear Reader,

This month, Silhouette Romance brings you six wonderful new love stories—guaranteed to keep your summer sizzling! Starting with a terrific FABULOUS FATHER by Arlene James. A *Mail-order Brood* was not what Leon Paradise was expecting when he asked Cassie Esterbridge to be his wife. So naturally the handsome rancher was shocked when he discovered that his mail-order bride came with a ready-made family!

Favorite author Suzanne Carey knows the kinds of stories Romance readers love. And this month, Ms. Carey doesn't disappoint. *The Male Animal* is a humorous tale of a couple who discover love—in the midst of their divorce.

The fun continues as Marie Ferrarella brings us another delightful tale from her Baby's Choice series—where matchmaking babies bring together their unsuspecting parents.

In an exciting new trilogy from Sandra Steffen, the Harris brothers vow that no woman will ever tie them down. But their WEDDING WAGER doesn't stand a chance against love. This month, a confirmed bachelor suddenly becomes a single father—and a more-than-willing groom—in *Bachelor Daddy*.

Rounding out the month, Jeanne Rose combines the thrill of the chase with the excitement of romance in *Love on the Run*. And *The Bridal Path* is filled with secrets—and passion—as Alaina Hawthorne spins a tale of love under false pretenses.

I hope you'll join us in the coming months for more great books from Elizabeth August, Kasey Michaels and Helen Myers.

Until then—

Happy Reading!

Anne Canadeo
Senior Editor

Please address questions and book requests to:
Silhouette Reader Service
U.S.: 3010 Walden Ave., P.O. Box 1325, Buffalo, NY 14269
Canadian: P.O. Box 609, Fort Erie, Ont. L2A 5X3

MOTHER ON THE WING

Marie Ferrarella

Silhouette
ROMANCE™
Published by Silhouette Books
America's Publisher of Contemporary Romance

To Nikky's best friend,
Jimmy Corbett,
for lending me
his brother and sister
and giving me a great line.
Thanks!

 SILHOUETTE BOOKS

ISBN 0-373-19026-3

MOTHER ON THE WING

Copyright © 1994 by Marie Rydzynski-Ferrarella

Printed in U.S.A.

MARIE FERRARELLA

was born in Europe, raised in New York City and now lives in Southern California. She describes herself as the tired mother of two overenergetic children and the contented wife of one wonderful man. She is thrilled to be following her dream of writing full-time.

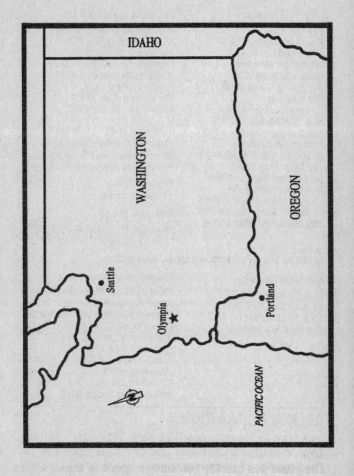

Prologue

They had no idea that they were going past her. Smiling to herself, Erin leaned over for a closer look as the small airplane whizzed by.

There she was again, the nice one. The one Erin had chosen for herself. The lady was talking to an elderly woman and saying something to make her smile. Erin could listen in if she wanted to, but for now she was content just to watch.

She had spent a lot of time watching the lady. But she had known right from the first.

She hugged herself, pleased. There was no doubt about it. Erin wanted the lady to be her mother. Wanted her even though she was always so busy.

Because busy as she was, the lady *always* had time for her two sons, Taylor and Stephen. Erin had watched the three of them together. Watched and yearned. In her little heart, she knew that the lady was just the kind of mother she wanted. One who could make every moment count.

The plane was quickly becoming a speck in the sky. This time, Erin chose to remain where she was rather than follow it. She had some serious planning to do. Her time was coming soon and she had to hurry if she wanted things to go her way.

If she wanted to choose her parents the way Jonathan had.

As a rule, it was forbidden to actively select your own parents. The Overseer had said so. The other angels had said so.

But rules were meant to be broken. They had since time began. Jonathan had succeeded in doing just that before her. He had selected his own parents and arranged for them to meet.

Erin smiled secretly to herself. Jonathan hadn't thought that anyone would know, but she did. She had watched him do it all.

And she had learned.

Parting a cloud with a wave of her tiny hand, Erin looked down and saw Jonathan. He was Jonathan Michaels now, and remembered nothing of what had come before. That was the price they each had to pay for gaining an earthly life. They had to forget their time here.

But it was a small price to pay for parents. Especially the right parents.

Erin concentrated and listened to him as he laughed in his playpen. No, Jonathan no longer recalled that he had broken all the rules and that, by doing so, he had become her example.

But it didn't matter. What mattered was that he had. And that she was going to.

Erin cocked her head and observed Jonathan as his uncle lifted him out of the playpen and began to play with him. She liked his uncle Frank.

Uncle Frank was really a lot of fun, she thought. He knew all the right games and he was never impatient or angry.

He was . . .

Perfect.

Erin's eyes lit up as she smiled again.

Yes, he was perfect.

Chapter One

The ride was a bumpy one. But then, the plane he was on was a great deal smaller than a 747. It was an ATR 42 belonging to an airline whimsically called Windsong and he was lucky to get on it. Otherwise, his trip to Seattle would have been delayed.

Not that Frank Harrigan was supposed to be in any particular hurry. For the first time in years, he was actually taking a vacation. And vacations were supposed to be laid-back. Yet he couldn't shake the sense of urgency he was experiencing. An urgency all the more strange because there was nothing to pin it to.

He wouldn't have been taking a vacation at all if it hadn't been for Greg's letter, coming to him completely out of the blue. That, and perhaps a premonition.

Funny how things managed to arrange themselves, he mused, like dancers moving to some mysterious song only they could hear. Three days ago, the letter had arrived from Greg Walters, someone he had all but lost touch with since he had graduated and returned to work at the clinic in Wilmington Falls. The letter had urged Frank to come to Seattle for a visit, to see the sights and renew old friendships.

The letter had gone on as if five years hadn't passed since they'd seen one another.

Frank had no idea why, but as he'd held Greg's letter in his hand, he'd felt this sudden urge to travel to Seattle. Unexpected, it had hit him with the force and intensity of a lightning bolt. It was so strong, so compelling, that he'd known he couldn't refuse it.

Instinctively, he also knew—though he had no idea *how* he knew—that he would have no peace until he went. And only regrets if he didn't. It was almost, he mused, as if he had an angel on his shoulder, whispering in his ear.

His curiosity aroused, Frank had decided to make arrangements to travel to Seattle. He had called Greg, who'd been excited to hear from him. Plans had quickly been formed. Frank would catch a shuttle to San Francisco and board another plane to Seattle. Greg would meet him at the airport.

It had seemed simple enough, if somewhat sudden.

Frank had waited until the last patient had left the clinic for the evening before he'd sprung the news on his sister. He had dropped it into the conversation as casually as if he was talking about buying a new pair of shoes....

Surprised, Jeannie shoved her hands deep into her lab coat and studied her brother in silence for a moment. He was older than she was by three years. As steadfast as a rock, Frank still had his unpredictable moments. This was obviously one of them.

Still, he'd been working hard for a long time now and heaven knew he deserved some time off. Between the two of them, they were the only medical assistance available in the area for over twenty miles. Everyone in Wilmington Falls came to them with everything from a hangnail to a nearly severed ear. The latter had been courtesy of a threshing machine.

"I would have thought, if anything, that you would have picked Las Vegas, with its bright lights and thin, long-legged women."

Frank grinned. "Sounds tempting, but I don't know anyone in Las Vegas."

Her brother was as gregarious as they came. "Never knew that to stop you before." Jeannie leaned a hip against the examining table. "So, tell me, have I ever met this Greg person?"

"I don't think so. He was someone I knew at school. I shared a dorm room with him." A memory rose before him. "Shared a few other things with him, as well." A grin formed that Jeannie thought best not to probe.

"I can't get over his writing to me out of the blue like this. We lost touch about five years ago." He rotated his shoulders, trying to work out a kink. It had been a long day. "I think I'm due for a vacation."

Jeannie nodded. "Way overdue."

Whatever else, he always knew that he could count on his sister for support. "Nice to hear you agree."

By the look on his face, she knew he was already making plans. "When are you leaving?"

"Friday."

He'd caught her by surprise again. "So soon? What's the rush?"

"I don't know," he admitted. "I just feel that there is."

He was being very mysterious, Jeannie thought. Frank never acted irrationally. There was always a basis—however remote and off-the-wall it might be—for his actions. It was actually part of his charm and what she had come to rely on years ago. She crossed her arms in front of her. There *had* to be a reason. Even as a child, there had always been reasons underscoring his whims.

"I don't understand."

Frank shrugged out of his lab coat and hung it on the hanger in the tiny closet in Jeannie's office. He picked up the nameplate on her desk. He had carved it for her himself when she'd graduated medical school. Jeanne Harrigan, M.D. Absently, he passed it from hand to hand, mulling over the questions they had in common.

He tried to find the words to explain the feelings to her as well as to himself. "You know how sometimes a person gets a premonition about things?"

The word *premonition* struck a chord so hard, Jeannie could almost feel it vibrate within her. It had been an irrepressible urge—a premonition so strong, it had overwhelmed her senses—that had compelled her to go to the lake the morning that she had first met her husband, Shane.

The incident was two years in the past now, but she remembered the feeling as clearly as if it had happened just this morning. It had felt as if she had no will of her own.

Thank God she hadn't fought it. Now Mollie had a father, and she had a wonderful husband and a baby boy that they all utterly adored. They had named him Jonathan, after Shane's late uncle Johnny.

"Yes, I do," she said softly.

Frank was deep in thought and didn't notice the change in his sister's voice. "Well, that's what this is. It's almost like 'go there and she will come.'"

Jeannie's head jerked up. "She?"

Frank looked at her blankly. "She? Did I say she?"

"You certainly did."

He shook his head. His mind had to be wandering, he thought. "I meant he. Greg. What else could I have meant?"

Jeannie smiled at him fondly. "You *are* overworked." She rose on her toes and kissed his forehead. "Go. Go to Seattle with my blessings and enjoy."

He certainly meant to do that, Frank thought, leaning back in his aisle seat, even if he'd gotten off to a rocky start. He'd boarded a plane at Riverdale's airport and had flown into San Francisco without any trouble. But then the ticket for his connecting flight had mysteriously vanished from his pocket and the clerk at the desk had had absolutely no record of him ever having made a reservation. And then the flight had been sold out.

Frustrated, bedeviled, it was just by happenstance that he'd glanced up at the departures/arrival board. There had been one departing flight for Seattle and it had been due to take off within the half hour.

Talk about luck.

Frank glanced to his right. There was no one sitting next to him and he had a clear view of what lay outside the tiny window. The sky had been steadily darkening as the flight progressed. He blinked. The cloud closest to him had an odd shape and reminded him of a small cherub.

Maybe they were flying too high, he thought, smiling to himself. The next instant, he noticed that the cloud was gone.

She could feel the turbulence seconds before it actually started. Ten years in the sky and she had a sixth sense about weather conditions. Donna McCullough could *feel* changes approaching.

The weather bureau had promised a beautiful day. A lot they knew, she thought. They were just a bunch of men with degrees in meteorology and a dart board.

She said a silent prayer, hoping that they would make the trip without incident. A licensed pilot, these days she rarely flew on the airline her father had left to her, unless one of the regular pilots couldn't make a run. But today was different. She was returning from the wedding of an old friend who'd moved to San Francisco. Weddings always made her weepy and sentimental.

And turbulence made her nervous.

Her planes were vigilantly maintained and kept in the best of condition, but fate was a funny thing and she never liked tempting it by feeling too confident. She had felt that way once, as if nothing could touch her. And then her world had come crashing down around her.

Donna couldn't wait until the plane landed in Seattle. She missed the boys. It had been only two days since she had seen them. It felt longer.

Maybe because it was nearing the anniversary of Tony's death, she thought with the same pang she always felt when remembering her late husband. When she thought of the waste it had been to have his life cut so short.

That was probably it. Ever since Tony had died two years ago, she had ceased to take even a moment of life for granted. Every hour away from Taylor and Stephen was an hour she could never replace.

Absently, she fingered the locket at her throat. Inside, she carried a picture of her sons. Her thoughts returned to them and she sighed. Taylor had been coming down with a cold when she left Wednesday. She had called her sister-in-law when the plane landed in San Francisco to see how he was doing. She'd talked to him, as well, but she wasn't going to be happy until she was there with him—even though he was eleven and "getting too big for baby stuff, Mom."

She smiled sadly to herself. They were small for such a short while.

Though it was a lot better now, her job still kept her away from them more than she would have liked. There were times when she seriously considered selling the charter service and getting a regular nine-to-five job, like a normal person. No more headaches about cargo shipments not arriving on time, no more trouble with the weather or disgruntled passengers who expected a sixteen-seater Albatross to fly as comfortably as a L1011. But the urge always passed quickly. Flying was in her blood.

Besides, until just recently, she wouldn't have gotten very much money for the company. Tony, with his head full of dreams, had overextended them by buying more small planes. He had mortgaged Windsong up to the hilt and then their business had hit a slump. Bill collectors had started appearing on her doorstep and they'd lost one of their ATRs. When Tony had died, he had left her with a mountain of bills and nothing but the charter service—and her own determination—to see her and the boys out of it.

She'd had to put in long hours at the office, finding ways to advertise cheaply, practically begging for business. She'd kept their remaining forty-seater flying one run from Seattle to San Francisco and back each day and the other small planes on lease for quick, private flights. She was the owner, manager and sales force all rolled into one. She couldn't afford to pay anyone else besides the flight crew and her mechanic. Maintaining the airplanes had sucked up everything but the barest minimum for them to live on. Fuel alone was exorbitant. The boys had been only four and nine when their father had died and back then she'd hated the idea of leaving them with strangers while she was away, but she hadn't had a choice.

Into the picture had come Tony's older sister, Lisa, a struggling lawyer with a huge heart. She had moved in—refusing to listen to a word of Donna's protest—to help out with the boys and the bills. Along with her had come Angelina, Lisa's soft-spoken part-time housekeeper who also doubled as a baby-sitter.

Somehow, life had eventually fallen into place and was even beginning to look up.

Knock wood, she mused inwardly.

As if to mock her, the plane suddenly lurched.

Used to bad weather, Donna still didn't quite manage to stifle her gasp as she grabbed the back of the seat closest to her. Her fingers slipped just as she lost her footing. Twisting around, Donna fell right onto the lap of one of the passengers. The one with the chiseled profile that she'd noticed almost immediately when he'd gotten on board.

"Oh, I'm so sorry."

The words tumbled out in a rush as Donna attempted to catch her breath. In the next moment, it seemed to whoosh out of her lungs again as she found herself looking up into the greenest eyes she'd ever seen.

Successfully masking his surprise, Frank automatically tightened his hand around the woman whom turbulence and heaven had seen fit to drop into his lap. His assessment was quick. She was petite, with deep brown hair and eyes the color of the sky they were flying in. And she felt as if she weighed next to nothing. Her bone structure looked to be excellent.

"I'm not."

Donna knew that the safest thing at the moment was not to allow herself to be drawn into a conversation. For some reason, his smile made her decidedly nervous. Ever the professional, she nevertheless smiled and quickly regained her feet. If her heart raced a little harder she told herself firmly, it was just the shock of falling that had caused it.

That, and the cologne he was wearing.

God, but it was sensual.

Donna quickly scanned the area. As she had suspected, the passengers were looking at one another uneasily.

"Just a little turbulence," she assured them. "Nothing to worry about." She had already introduced herself to several of the passengers. Donna liked to maintain a hands-on attitude about her airline and field complaints immediately. Her first concern was always passenger satisfaction.

She had a sneaking suspicion that she knew what *this* passenger's satisfaction involved. Maybe that was why there had been, what felt like, an electrical shock crackling between them for that brief instant.

She turned to walk away, but the man she had just shared space with seemed to have other ideas on the matter. He caught her wrist, tethering her momentarily. Donna looked down at him quizzically, wondering if she was going to have any trouble with the man. It had been a long time since there had been an incident with a male passenger. At the time, it had involved a man who had done just a shade too much partying on the ground. He had wandered into the cockpit to see for himself that the plane was being piloted by a woman.

He'd asked her if she wanted to try flying another way once they landed. Rafferty, her copilot, had been quick to set him straight.

Looking into this man's eyes, she decided that there would be no need for Rafferty, who was flying the plane now, to come out to speak with him. Despite the mischievous glint in the passenger's gaze, there was something gentle there, too.

"You're not hurt, are you?"

She was surprised at the question and relaxed a little, though her countenance never changed. "I'd say neither one of us is the worse for wear."

It was the oddest thing, Frank thought, but for the split second the woman had been on his lap, he had had the feeling that *this*—not Greg's invitation—was the reason he had

thrown his clothes into the suitcase he'd borrowed from
Jeannie and had boarded the plane.

The next moment had him shrugging away the thought.

His smile was wide and easy. It slipped right over Donna's skin, as smoothly as a drop of expensive body lotion.
"I wouldn't bet on it."

It was a line and she knew it. Heaven knew she had heard
more than her share of them. But it had been so smoothly
and so genuinely delivered that Donna had to give him
points for it. The man seemed affable enough, though she
was certain with a face like his, he was used to women falling into his lap with a fair amount of regularity. She wondered if he thought she had done it on purpose.

Donna squared her shoulders.

"If you're hurt, you can always file a claim with our insurance company. I'm Donna McCullough, and Windsong
is happy to serve you whenever it can." On that cheerful
note, Donna gently extracted her wrist from his grasp.

Without giving the dark-haired passenger a second glance,
she began to make her way down the aisle to check on the
other passengers. Since there was no flight attendant on
board, Donna would have to do what she could to assuage
any of their fears.

She hoped that the air pocket they'd hit was just that and
not the beginning of something worse. Donna widened her
smile, hoping that would dispel any possible concern on the
part of the passengers.

"Is this usual?" The question came from a young mother
on her right. She was traveling with a girl of about ten.

"There's really no reason for concern. We—" Donna got
no further. She felt someone grab her wrist from the other
side. She turned around, fully expecting to see the dark-
haired man again.

But this time, Donna found herself looking down into a
pair of terrified brown eyes. They were set in the round face
of a woman who couldn't have been older than twenty.
Perhaps not even that. Her other hand was splayed protec-
tively over her belly. The woman was noticeably pregnant.

"Miss?" The single word was full of terror as it tumbled from the young woman's lips.

Donna covered the woman's hand with her free one, gently attempting to pry the fingers from her wrist. "It's all right," she said soothingly. "We'll be in Seattle soon." For a little thing, she certainly had a death grip, Donna thought.

The young blonde's lower lip bore the imprint of fresh teeth marks. She shook her head and her bangs bobbed back and forth, a few hairs sticking to her damp forehead.

"No, it's not that, it's—" Each word was being forced out as if it were being pushed through a strainer whose holes were too small to allow passage. "My water," she began again. "It broke fifteen minutes ago and—" The blonde didn't finish and tears created by pain instantly sprang to her eyes. "I think—I think— Oh, help me, please—" she managed to cry out.

As the words gushed forth, Donna felt the woman's grip tighten to the point that she became aware of her own pulse throbbing. The plane shuddered again like a mountain climber losing his footing. Turbulence was getting worse.

Oh, God, when it rains, it pours.

Donna had to concentrate on keeping her smile fixed as she looked at the woman. "It'll be fine."

But the woman had visibly paled. "It doesn't feel so fine." Her eyes were a little wild as she appealed to Donna. "I'm not due for another month."

Whatever else the woman was going to say was blocked off when she uttered a tiny animal cry. It sounded as if she were a puppy, whimpering.

Donna looked around the small space. The plane had forty seats in all and most of them were filled. She saw curiosity and concern, but no help. "Is there a doctor aboard?"

It sounded like an absurd line from a B movie. But doctors flew like everyone else. Donna sincerely hoped that one was flying today and that he or she was on this plane.

To her surprise, she saw the man whose lap she had fallen into making his way down the aisle toward them. He was holding onto the seats on either side of him, as if anticipating another lunge at any moment.

I said a doctor, not someone who wants to play *doctor,* Donna thought in a flash of frustrated irritation.

"Are you a doctor?" Donna knew the answer before it was given.

"No."

Then why was he wasting their time? Did he enjoy seeing pain up close and personal? Her smile grew frosty around the edges. "Then please return to your—"

"I'm a nurse." Frank interrupted her dismissal. "Is there a problem?"

Donna looked at the dark-haired man skeptically, but the pregnant woman was gripping her hand so tightly now, she could feel nails sinking into her flesh.

"She's—" Donna didn't have to bother completing her statement.

"Oh." He immediately saw the pain and panic in the woman's eyes, as well as her condition. It hadn't been evident from his position a moment ago. Frank crouched down to be level with the seated woman. When he spoke, it was in a calm, soothing voice. "Are you having contractions?"

The woman nodded and swallowed before attempting to answer. "I'm early. This isn't supposed to be happening." Pain strangled every breath she took. "But my water broke."

Frank had hoped that perhaps the unexpected turbulence and decidedly bumpy ride had brought on a feeling of premature labor. But if her water had broken, this was obviously the real thing.

Laying a comforting hand on her shoulder, Frank looked into her terrified eyes. "What's your name?"

"Rosemary. Rosemary D'Angelo." Taking a deep breath, she released her hold on Donna.

Frank glanced down and saw that the woman's wedding ring was cutting into her flesh. He wondered where her husband was at a time like this. But all that was moot. What mattered was her condition.

"All right, Rosemary, we're going to make you as comfortable as possible."

Her eyes darted back and forth like tiny blackberries being shaken in a jar. "Here?"

Frank's smile never faded. "It's a very nice airplane." Rising, he looked at Donna. He lowered his voice a little. "Have any training?"

Donna shrugged, feeling somewhat helpless. This wasn't something that had been covered in the instruction manual when she'd taken up flying, initially at her father's behest. "No."

He nodded, resigned. "All right, the main thing is that you don't faint on me."

Her eyes held his for a moment. Donna felt some sort of a challenge being silently issued. Her eyes narrowed. "I don't faint."

"Fine."

Another minor ripple shook the plane. Donna automatically grabbed the man's shoulder to steady herself. Quickly she dropped her hand to her side. "What do you want me to do?"

Offhand, Frank could think of a couple of things that he would enjoy, but they had absolutely nothing to do with the woman who needed them both right now. And she was his first priority.

"Move the passengers in the front to other seats. We're going to need the room. And if you've got any blankets, put a couple on the floor for a pallet, and use the rest to form a curtain. I'm sure the lady would like some privacy." He stopped only to smile reassuringly at Rosemary. "How much longer before we land in Seattle?"

As if on cue, the intercom went on, preceded with a squawk that bore testimony to the increasingly inclement weather. "Ladies and gentlemen, this is your captain speaking. There's an unexpected storm ahead. The flight tower has advised us to detour to the Lakeview, Oregon, airport in order to avoid it." The man's voice was deep and calm. "This is just standard procedure and there is nothing to worry about."

Something was wrong, Donna thought. Lakeview Airport wasn't one they would normally reroute to.

Nothing to worry about, eh? "Easy for him to say," Frank muttered, glancing toward the pale woman who now held on to his hand as if it were her lifeline.

He looked at Donna again. So much for turning this problem over to a medical team. "Well, that answers that. Just get the blankets."

She nodded and hurried off. Her first stop was going to be the cockpit. Rafferty needed to be apprised of the situation out here. And she needed to be apprised of the situation in the cockpit.

Frank turned to Rosemary. He was as composed in appearance as if he were sitting at Sally's Restaurant back home, sharing a warm apple pie and a few stories with his friends. "Rosemary, my name is Frank Harrigan, and I've delivered twenty-seven babies. This is going to be number twenty-eight." He winked at her. "And it's going to be a snap. Trust me."

Perspiration had plastered the rest of her bangs to her forehead by now. Rosemary looked dubious about the assurance, but she had to cling to something. She licked her lips. "I'm not afraid."

"That's my girl." Frank enveloped her hand in both of his.

Donna emerged from the cockpit and tried to calm herself. The news wasn't good. In addition to the storm, the fuel gauge was registering half a tank, which was impossible. They'd started at completely full, as always, and they hadn't gone that far. She was betting that the fuel gauge was broken for some reason, but she couldn't risk being wrong. Donna tried not to think of the possible consequences of that. There was a new life struggling to come into the world. This was no time to think of death.

She shuddered, anyway.

Moving quickly, Donna took down the five blankets she kept stacked in an overhead compartment in case anyone requested one. Laying three on the floor, she managed, with the aid of some twine and a resourceful passenger, to hastily string up the other two to form a curtain. The passengers in the front obligingly shifted to the rear of the plane. Several owlishly watched the darkening sky outside their windows.

Donna returned to Frank. "I've cleared off an area."

Frank nodded and rose to his feet. "All right. Help me with Rosemary."

Her knees weak with anticipation, spasms of pain sporadically dancing through her, Rosemary felt she was in no condition to move.

"I don't think I can stand."

Panic was beginning to freeze her up, Frank thought. "Sure you can. It's only a few feet away," he promised her, his voice as soothing as if he were speaking to his year-old nephew.

Frank gently coaxed Rosemary to her feet. Clutching at him, she cried out as more pain shot through her. He quickly wrapped his arm around her back.

"Hold on," he warned. And then to Donna's surprise, he picked the woman up in his arms.

The aisle between the two rows of seats was small. It certainly wasn't designed for a six-foot man carrying a pregnant woman to pass through easily. But somehow Frank managed the short distance to the front of the compartment.

Donna pulled back the makeshift khaki curtain she and the passenger had put up.

Frank carefully placed Rosemary on the blanket, then pulled the curtain closed. The last thing he needed was someone kibitzing and offering their advice. He smiled down at Rosemary. "This is going to be a private party. By invitation only."

Rosemary tried to smile in return, but it was evident to Donna that the young girl was terrified. The smile was nothing more than merely a weak quiver of her lips. He took the pregnant woman's hand and wrapped his fingers around hers firmly, as if willing his strength into her.

"Is this your first?" he asked softly.

Rosemary could only nod in reply as another contraction seized her.

Because of her age and the look of sheer terror in her eyes, Frank had suspected as much. "There's nothing to be afraid of." Holding her hand against his chest, he continued to smile down at the young woman. "This is the best time of your life, you know," he informed her solemnly. "You're still in charge. Once you push them out, they have a mind of their own and do pretty much what they want."

Rosemary almost shriveled up into herself as the contraction passed. Her face was already racked with exhaustion. "Do you have any children?"

He shook his head. "No, but my sister does. Two." When he began to draw his hand away from hers, he saw fear reenter her eyes. He nodded to the tiny lavatory behind them. "I'm just going to wash up, Rosemary." He rose to his feet. "I'll be back as soon as I can."

Rosemary bit down on her lip as another contraction began.

"Stay with her," Frank told Donna.

"I wasn't planning on making a break for it," Donna answered quietly as she sank down beside Rosemary. Donna didn't care for the fact that the man felt he had to tell her to remain. Pure compassion—if nothing else—would have made her stay.

She knew she was being edgy. The storm was partially responsible for that. That, and her concern about the fuel. She thought of her boys and her heart swelled. Silently she promised them that she would be home soon. And then she turned her attention to the woman on the floor.

Some vacation. As Frank rinsed his hands in the rest room, he watched the water swirl down the metal basin, announcing its departure with a continuous gurgle. Maybe this was the reason for the sudden urgency to take Greg up on his invitation and travel to Seattle, he mused. Maybe there was some vast design that had put him here at this time to help Rosemary have her baby.

He had never been very religious to begin with, but it made sense to him.

Things, he thought, always happened for a reason.

Rosemary's sharp cry had Frank running back before he could dry off his hands. Water was dripping from them as he looked questioningly at Donna.

Rosemary almost reared from the mound of blankets. "I think it's coming."

False alarms were coming. He sank down next to her, gently brushing the damp hair from her face. "Rosemary, the first time it usually takes—"

She moved her head from side to side, vehemently denying his statement before he could complete it. "I don't care about usually. I can feel it coming."

Well, experience or not, she was in a better position to know than he was. After all, it was her body. Frank nodded as he took the hem of her flowered dress in his hand. There was no polite way to do this.

His eyes remained on Rosemary's face as he began to lift her dress. "I'm going to have to see how far you're dilated, Rosemary."

Rosemary was past embarrassment. Waves of pain had washed it from her.

"Anything," she cried. "Anything. Just help me, please."

Donna's own two deliveries had been almost sinfully simple, but she could feel Rosemary's pain. Holding the woman's other hand, Donna tried to absorb some of it herself.

She looked at Frank over Rosemary's head. "Don't you have anything to give her?"

He hadn't even thought of bringing along his medical bag. This wasn't supposed to be a working vacation. And it wasn't as if he were a doctor.

Yet now he wished he *had* packed his bag along with his clothes.

He shook his head. "I hadn't planned on delivering a baby at thirty thousand feet. Best I can suggest is a shot of Scotch."

"We don't carry any liquor on this flight." And for the first time, she regretted that.

"No, no," Rosemary protested weakly, not even hearing Donna. "I want everything clear. I—" The sentence ended in a guttural screech and she arched her body.

Frank dropped the hem. She was almost fully dilated. Mercifully, he thought, it wouldn't be long now.

"Donna?" Rafferty's voice came from the cockpit. "Is there anything I can do?"

"It's all right," Frank called out without even looking up. "Everything's under control." His eyes were on Rosemary's. "You're almost ready to push, Rosemary."

Donna felt a sudden wave of nausea flitter through her. "Just keep the plane level, Rafferty," she called back over her shoulder.

Frank glanced at Donna. "You have a very commanding presence. Think you can order this baby out—fast?"

If she could've, she would've. Donna watched helplessly as another spasm of pain began to envelop Rosemary. The woman's face contorted. "Unfortunately, my authority extends only to adults. My two sons do whatever they want."

She was married.

Frank had no idea why, in the middle of the drama that was playing itself out before him, that single thought made him feel so disappointed.

But it did.

Chapter Two

Frank had no time to dwell on the disappointment he felt or on any extraneous thought that might, in some way, interfere with what he had to do. What he needed to do. Rosemary was almost writhing on the floor before him.

Her face a mask of mingled pain and panic, Rosemary was arching upward. Her entire upper body weight was resting on her elbows. It was as if, somehow, she were trying to eject the baby from her. Blankets became scrambled and bunched beneath her as she moved.

Donna made soothing noises as she encouraged Rosemary to relax. She gently pressed the pregnant woman back on the floor. She used the same tone she employed with Stephen when thunderstorms brought the little boy running into her bedroom at night.

The next moment Rosemary was pulling her elbows in until they practically dug into her rib cage. Her eyes were opened wide, alert. Frank recognized the signs. She was going to push.

He placed a gentling hand on her shoulder. "No, not yet, Rosemary. Don't push. It's too soon."

But Rosemary shook her head from side to side, pain eating away at her energy. The motion was all the argument she could manage. "The baby wants to come out. *Now*."

Frank checked quickly. She wasn't dilated far enough, and if she bore down now, she would only succeed in tearing herself. He had no way to rectify that. No surgical needle, no sutures. Nothing.

He refrained from dragging his hand through his hair in frustration. God, he wished Jeannie was here, or at least her ever-present medical bag.

"Breathe, Rosemary, breathe."

Tears were spilling down Rosemary's cheeks. Her eyes begged him for help as she looked up. "I *am* breathing."

She didn't understand. Frank shook his head. "No, like this." His eyes holding hers, Frank very deliberately expelled air through pursed lips. The sound was hypnotically rhythmic.

The look in Rosemary's eyes became wild as the urgency to push mounted, barreling through her body with the force of a freight train.

"It won't help—" she cried, frightened. "I have to push."

Frank's expression never wavered. "Do it," he ordered firmly.

Donna looked at him in surprise. She wouldn't have guessed that he could sound so stern.

Like the child she had been such a short time go, Rosemary obeyed. Clutching Donna's hand, she imitated the sound that Frank had made. He joined her. The rhythm of their breathing blended until the urge to push left her. Rosemary slumped back against the blankets like a limp rag doll.

Ever so lightly, Frank stroked damp hair away from Rosemary's forehead. "Contraction over." It wasn't a question as much as a reassuring statement.

Her lips moved weakly. "Yes." The next moment, she was tensing again. Her eyes darted to Frank's face. "I think—"

He knew. "—there's another one coming." Praying, Frank examined Rosemary again. The relief he experienced was for the both of them. In the space of a few minutes, she had become fully dilated. He had no explanation for it, but it had obviously happened. "All right, Rosemary, this time, I want you to push."

Rosemary almost cried. It was going to be over, finally over. "I'm ready?"

He nodded. "You're ready." Frank only hoped that he was.

The plane shuddered. The storm, no doubt. Donna could feel Rosemary's panic mounting. She placed a soothing hand on her shoulder, murmuring to her again. Donna looked at Frank. "What do you want me to do?"

"Get behind her. I want you to raise her shoulders up and support her when I tell her to push." Donna shifted and prayed that the landing would be swift and smooth.

Rosemary caught her breath as a contraction began to roll over her with the intensity of a bulldozer. Her eyes flew wide open again and she dug her nails into the blankets beneath her. One curved pink tip went flying.

"Ahh—!"

This was it. "Now, Rosemary. Push!" Frank ordered, his hands ready to ease out the infant.

Heat radiated through the blankets. Donna could feel the woman's back tensing, could feel her steely concentration as Rosemary struggled to push her child into the world.

Frank raised his eyes to Rosemary's face. Perspiration dripping into her watery eyes, she was the portrait of exhaustion. "Okay, rest."

On cue, Rosemary slumped against Donna's hands, panting heavily. She couldn't seem to gulp in enough air.

"You're doing fine." Donna's voice was soft, covering her growing concern that the baby hadn't emerged yet. "Just fine."

Donna raised her eyes to Frank's, searching for any contradiction to her words. The only births she'd attended were those of her sons. They had passed so quickly, the entire process was a blur. She had no idea if things were progressing well or if there was a problem.

Frank spared her a short nod. His attention was centered on Rosemary. He watched the pregnant woman's face for signs of the next contraction. He didn't have to wait long.

Though Rosemary gritted her teeth together, a sharp, piercing cry emerged.

Frank was ready, offering up a short prayer that this would truly be it. "Show time, Rosemary. Maybe we'll get lucky this time, eh?" He flashed her a broad smile.

Rosemary licked her dry lips and barely nodded. "Maybe," she agreed hoarsely.

The next moment Rosemary was hunched forward, her shoulders pulled together as if they were two conspirators, huddling in secrecy. She gave the appearance of attempting to squeeze the baby out.

When Rosemary fell back, gasping, too tired to sob, Frank motioned Donna over to the side. By his estimation, they had about a minute before the next contraction took hold. Maybe less. He looked over his shoulder at Rosemary, but she seemed too exhausted to notice that he had left her side.

"How much longer before we land?" he asked in a low voice.

Donna saw the look of concern in his eyes, the look he was trying to hide from Rosemary. *Was* something going wrong? "Fifteen minutes."

Fifteen minutes. Frank doubted that Rosemary could go on like this for another fifteen minutes or so. She looked too frail to continue pushing much longer. "Has the pilot—?"

Donna was nodding before he had a chance to finish his question. "He's already radioed ahead for an ambulance. They'll have one standing by when we land."

That did Rosemary precious good right now, he thought contrarily. "Meanwhile, back at the ranch—" Frank muttered, exasperated.

Donna placed a hand on his arm. She could see he was worried. "Is she in any real danger?" She felt her throat constricting as she whispered the question.

"I'm not sure. The baby should be out by now. She's not strong enough to keep this up for very long. Got any miracles up your sleeve?" He turned to look at Rosemary. It was almost time for another one.

"I—" Donna began.

Rosemary's shoulders had tensed. *Here we go again,* Frank thought, quickly squatting down and repositioning himself.

Rosemary's eyes, wild, searched for Frank. "Frank—?"

"Right here, honey. I'm not going anywhere until I know if it's a boy or girl," he told her conversationally. "I love mysteries, don't you?"

He sounded so casual, so calm, Donna thought. But she saw the thin bead of perspiration across his brow.

Rosemary was chewing her lower lip so hard, it was bleeding. "I can't—"

He couldn't let her give up. He had no recourse to offer her. "Yes, you can and you will." The words were gentle, but firm. It was as if he were willing a transfusion of strength and courage into the frail woman. "You'll do whatever it takes because you want to see this baby born even more than I do."

Recalling every pep talk he'd ever given on any subject, Frank went on talking to Rosemary. He only hoped that he could convince her not to cave in.

Donna could feel herself being mesmerized by the sound of Frank's voice as he coached Rosemary through the waves of pain to the end of her goal. They tried twice more. Each time, Rosemary grew weaker and more despondent.

Her own throat dry, Donna propped Rosemary up yet again as another contraction began. Donna's fingers were tense and cramping up beneath the blanket. Frank continued talking, urging, coaxing.

It seemed like an eternity later when, with a piercing shriek from Rosemary, the baby emerged into the world. Donna felt like crying and laughing at the same time.

That had to be the hardest birth he had ever witnessed, Frank thought. Mavis Turner had had a difficult time with her third, but Jeannie had opted for a cesarean long before Mavis was as drained as Rosemary. There was blood all over the blankets. Frank could only hope that Donna was right in her estimation of when they would land. Rosemary needed more professional care than he could give her.

But right now, he felt like celebrating. He was holding a brand-new life in his hands. It never ceased to awe him.

"You did it," Frank cried softly. "You did it, Rosemary. You have a beautiful baby girl."

After sterilizing his pocket knife over a match flame, Frank cut the cord. He carefully wiped the tiny face with his own handkerchief. Gently he wrapped the child in a blanket and placed her in her mother's arms.

"Beautiful," he repeated, leaning back on his heels. "Just like her mother."

Donna let out a long sigh of relief. She thought she had never seen anything quite so movingly tender as the look on Frank's face when he handed Rosemary her child.

Their eyes met and held for a moment and not a sound was heard around them. In that one instant, Donna had the eeriest feeling that Frank was privy to her thoughts. It was a feeling that was eerie and yet oddly stirring at the same time.

Frank felt suddenly and completely drained himself. He ran his hand through his damp hair, then smiled at Donna. Odd how, throughout the whole ordeal, he had been aware of the faint scent of her perfume. "You're pretty good under pressure."

As unobtrusively as possible, Donna tried to replace the most soaked blanket under Rosemary with a clean one. "I could say the same for you."

He flashed a smile that Donna found particularly disarming. "I'm a country boy," he told her, rising. There was blood on his hands and his shirt, and a smear across his jeans along his thighs. He looked pretty disheveled, he thought. He was going to have to find a way to change before they landed in Seattle. "We know how to improvise."

Though he was bone-weary, Frank realized that he also felt energized. And immensely satisfied with himself and the world at large.

There was no way to remove the bloodied blanket without disturbing Rosemary. Donna gave up. The paramedics would be here as soon as they landed. Then Rosemary would have clean sheets as well as a clean blanket.

Donna glanced at Frank. "Do you know you're grinning from ear to ear?" She found it vastly appealing.

"I always do when things go right." He winked at Rosemary. Then he looked down at the mess on the floor. The two top blankets were ruined—he'd used one to wrap up the placenta—and there was blood on the rug, as well. "I think the airline is going to have to do a bit of cleaning before your next passengers will want to use these blankets."

Donna wiped her forehead with the back of her hand. Just a short while ago, she'd been cold. Amazing what a little tension could do to raise your body heat.

She looked out the window. The storm looked as though it was abating and they were descending. They'd be landing soon. Thank God.

"I'll worry about it when we land." Frank looked at her oddly, wondering what she meant by that. He'd already figured out that she was with Windsong in some capacity. Did her duties entail cleaning up, too?

Donna bent down next to Rosemary. "Is there anything I can get for you?"

Rosemary shook her head. Her heart and her arms were full. It was right there in her eyes for them to see. With fingers that were still awkward, she brushed back the tiny tuft of hair on her daughter's head. "This will do nicely."

Donna remembered what it had felt like to hold her firstborn in her arms. Like heaven. And the weight of that responsibility had been both frightening and exhilarating. She would have given anything to get that time back. Tony had still been alive then.

Donna forced a smile to her lips. "You have the distinction of being the first woman to give birth on Windsong Airlines." The smile came a little more naturally now. "So, what are you going to call her?"

Rosemary deliberated for a moment before turning her eyes up to Frank. Frank stopped rolling down his sleeve and raised a questioning brow. Rosemary smiled at him. "Frankie."

Donna nodded her approval as she rose to her feet. "Looks like you've got a namesake."

Frank laughed. The next moment, the plane lurched and Donna fell against him. He was quick to catch her, quick to tighten his arms around her again. Yet, looking down into her upturned face, something tightened within *him*, like the string on a violin bow just before a concert. "This is a habit I could enjoy getting used to."

Donna flushed as she pushed herself out of his arms. "I seem to have lost my air legs."

Because she seemed flustered, Frank shifted his gaze to the woman on the floor. He was aware of Donna moving to the tiny lavatory as he bent down and placed his hand over Rosemary's on the baby.

"Now that she has my name, we're going to have to stay in touch." His expression grew serious. "Is there anyone you want me to call when we land?"

Rosemary shut her eyes for a moment as tears suddenly formed. When she opened them again, they spilled out, refusing to stay trapped in her soul.

"Daniel. We had a fight and I went to stay with my mother. He doesn't know I'm coming back," she added quickly. "Tell him I'm sorry." She smiled at the baby dozing in her arms. "And tell him he has a daughter. He'll like that."

Frank's legs were aching from crouching for so long, but he sank down next to her again. "I'll need a number."

Rosemary nodded. "He's in Seattle. Daniel D'Angelo. He's my husband."

"I had my suspicions." He looked up in surprise when Donna handed him a pad and pencil. Beautiful, didn't rattle under pressure and efficient. And married, he reminded himself sternly, wishing he didn't feel this strong wave of attraction to her. "Thanks."

Donna nodded. She'd brought back a cold towel to wipe the perspiration from Rosemary's face. Rosemary sighed audibly as the cloth touched her skin. "I left him. It was a stupid argument and I shouldn't have run out. Tell him I know that now."

Anticipating the reconciliation, Rosemary smiled as she told Frank her husband's telephone number, then added the address for good measure.

Just as Frank tucked away the note into his back pocket, the captain's voice came over the loudspeaker. "Ladies and gentlemen, we'll be landing in Lakeview in a few minutes. The delay shouldn't be too long."

Donna certainly hoped not. Lakeview's airport was a small one. If for some reason they *were* running low on fuel, she hoped they could get some more quickly. If it was the fuel gauge itself, that shouldn't be a problem to ascertain. But for now at least they were landing in one piece.

And their number had increased by one. She smiled at the sleeping newborn.

". . . we're sorry for this inconvenience," the captain was concluding. "And we thank you for flying Windsong Airlines."

Donna sighed. *And hope you won't change airlines after this.* She tossed the wet hand towel aside. "God, I hate delays."

With a short, sharp pang that surprised him, Frank envisioned her getting off the plane in Seattle and running into the arms of a tall, eminently happy-looking man. "In a hurry to get home?" he asked casually.

Donna hadn't realized that she'd said the words out loud. Looking at Frank, she nodded. "Yes. I don't like leaving my boys alone too long."

He wondered if she was one of those overprotective mothers. His own had let him roam free. She hadn't had much of a choice, actually. He'd been headstrong and more than a handful when he was younger, positive he was right about everything. Lucky for him his mother had been so understanding. And so patient.

"Aren't they with your husband?" He knew it was absolutely none of his business who they were with. But he also knew that he had to ask, so that he could satisfy himself about her marital status one final time.

Donna's face sobered, though she tried to hide it. "I'm a widow."

The words always hurt, even now, after so much time had gone by. She was Tony's widow. The thought stung like nettles being pulled across her palm. She wondered if the pain would ever fade away completely. Or the guilt.

He had no right to feel happy over her sorrow, and yet there was a tiny ray of sunshine that sprang up in his chest. She was a widow.

She wasn't married.

Still, it wouldn't go over very well if he grinned. Restraining himself, he said, "I'm sorry, I didn't mean to bring up a sensitive subject."

Donna shrugged away his words. She shouldn't have become personal with a passenger in the first place. But the circumstances in this case, she mused, glancing at the woman and infant on the floor, *were* extenuating.

"Apology accepted."

The seat belt sign to her left began to flash. They were landing, she thought. And none too soon.

"At least that's working," she muttered. Donna looked at Frank. "You'd better go strap in."

Donna couldn't leave Rosemary, and there was no way the young mother could sit up in a seat.

She knelt beside Rosemary. With luck, there wouldn't be a problem landing, but just in case, she wanted to make certain that Rosemary was made as comfortable as possible.

"Don't worry, I'll be right here," she assured her.

"We both will."

Donna glanced up in time to see Frank kneeling down at Rosemary's other side. He lightly placed his hand on her arm, prepared to hold her in place if necessary.

"If you don't mind, I'd just as soon join you on the floor." He was addressing Donna, but he was looking at Rosemary as he spoke. The young woman was paler than he would have liked. "This looks like a new way to hold a séance. How are you feeling, Rosemary?"

"Wonderful." Though they were sparkling, her eyes were almost half closed from fatigue. "Thanks to you. I would have really panicked," she confided, "if you hadn't been here."

Donna could have testified to that. The woman had been halfway there when Frank had appeared and taken over.

But Frank merely shook his head, contradicting her statement. "You would have done just fine."

Rosemary looked unconvinced.

As soon as the plane touched down and opened its doors, the paramedics hurried on board, pushing a gurney in front of them. With swift, capable hands, they transferred Rosemary and her baby from the floor and onto the mobile stretcher. Frank filled them in quickly, then asked the taller of the two men the name of the hospital where she was being taken. He intended to check on her after they landed in Seattle. He didn't like leaving things half-done. Besides, he knew her husband would want to know.

Donna listened silently. He sounded, she thought, as if he really cared. She wondered if he was being sincere, or if he was just a very good actor. In either case, it obviously made Rosemary feel better, and that was what counted.

"You won't forget?" Rosemary asked, raising her voice as she was being whisked away. "About calling Daniel?"

Frank pulled the notepaper from his back pocket and held it aloft as the paramedics hurried down the aisle in the gurney. "I won't forget," he promised.

The people on either side of the aisle stared as the paramedics guided Rosemary and her baby off the plane.

"That should take care of your good deeds through the end of the year," Donna commented.

Frank returned the note to his pocket. "All in a day's work where I come from."

"Speaking of work..."

Donna's voice trailed off as she went toward the exit. She intended to see each passenger off with a reassuring word. So far, they hadn't seemed disgruntled by the delay. She wanted to make sure it stayed that way.

Frank hung back, taking a seat. Perhaps it was the little drama they had both been inadvertently pulled into, perhaps it was something else entirely, but he felt close to her. Close and immensely intrigued. He knew he wanted to learn more about this petite brunette with the flashing blue eyes.

Donna saw him sitting and wondered why he hadn't gotten off yet.

"Sitting here won't make the plane fly," she said as she approached him. Inexplicably, tension suddenly rose up through her shoulders.

"I know. I was waiting for you." He rose, and she was suddenly aware of how much taller he was than she. She hadn't had time to notice that before. He tipped an imaginary hat. "Walk you into the airport, ma'am?"

The tension left as suddenly as it had come. "I need to have a word with the pilot first."

Frank inclined his head. "I can wait." He grinned and spread his hands. "I don't have anywhere to go."

Donna went to the cockpit, wishing that she didn't feel so oddly unsettled. Undoubtedly, it was just everything coming together at once, not the color of his eyes that was getting to her.

"Rafferty." She poked her head into the small cockpit. "See if you can get anyone to check the fuel gauge for us, and the fuel tanks, too." She tapped the gauge on the instrument panel. "That doesn't make sense."

"You're telling me." A silver-haired man in his fifties, Rafferty pursed his lips in a thoughtful frown. "And we're miles away from the Bermuda Triangle."

She grinned. "Your sense of direction isn't *that* bad. Get back to me when you find a mechanic. I'll be in the terminal, calling home."

"Gotcha, boss lady."

"Ooh, I do like the sound of that." She laughed. It was a standard, harmless flirtation they always exchanged. Rafferty was happily married and she had made up her mind to stay widowed. There wasn't going to be any other man for her—ever. She didn't want there to be. The emotional price tag was far too high to pay.

He was waiting for her when she emerged.

He saw the surprised look on her face. "Forget about me?" he guessed.

Donna shook her head. "Not a chance." The trouble was she had a feeling, a strange foreshadowing, that she was right.

The airport was crammed. It wasn't built to handle passengers on any large scale. Theirs wasn't a large plane, but it wasn't a small one, either and the terminal's complement of fifty-five seats was almost filled. Donna walked in just ahead of Frank and hoped that the airport had a mechanic around. One they could get to quickly.

The first thing she had to do, now that she had assigned Rafferty to find the mechanic, was to let Lisa know she was going to be a great deal later than either of them would like.

She looked around for a telephone and saw three along the far wall. There was a huge crowd in front of all of them. Naturally.

She sighed.

Frank saw where she was looking. "We could try sending smoke signals."

For a moment, she'd forgotten that he was behind her. Oh well, the crowd was bound to thin out eventually. She looked at him. "Do you always get perfect strangers to trust you like that?" Crossing her arms, Donna resigned herself to waiting. Being anxious wouldn't help anything.

She saw that Frank had taken out the paper with Rosemary's husband's telephone number on it. He was going to call the man just as he had promised. Donna was impressed. After all, he was under no obligation to Rosemary, or to Daniel, for that matter.

People had always trusted him. He had a knack of getting them to open up. It had never taken any effort on his part, but saying so would sound like bragging, so he restricted himself to smiling in answer to her question. Then he added, "Only the ones whose babies I help deliver."

The level of noise was rising and swelling all around them in the airport. Being stranded in an airport in the middle of nowhere wasn't much of a homecoming.

He saw someone in royal blue overalls hurrying to confer with a frowning older man Frank took to be the pilot of their downed plane. "So, how long do you think we're going to be here?"

There were standard, vague answers to that question, but Donna believed that Frank deserved more than that. "Honestly?"

He liked the way her eyebrows rose when she asked questions. He inclined his head in a gesture of conspiracy. "I'd expect nothing less from someone I've just shared life's greatest miracle with."

Their eyes held for a second and it was as if she had just had a vision of what was to come. It was odd, but she couldn't shake the feeling. Her laugh was therefore tinged with an edginess she couldn't account for. "I'm not sure. There's something wrong with our fuel gauge."

Cars and planes were only machines at bottom and he knew evasiveness when he heard it. "Does that mean we're losing fuel?"

"No," she replied firmly, "that means there's something wrong with our fuel gauge." *I hope.*

"Is that all?"

Was he pumping her? she wondered, half-amused. "Yes. Why?"

"You were white when you returned from the cockpit and I didn't think it was because the pilot had made a pass." The man, Frank judged, wouldn't have dared. Though she was small, she gave every indication of being able to hold her own. This was a woman men sought out as a friend and made passes at only once they were assured that they would be willingly received.

She would have liked to think that she was better at masking her thoughts than that. The line to the telephone moved a little and she inched her way forward. "I've been flying for ten years now. I'm not supposed to turn white. It must have been the lightning." For some reason, perhaps because of the way he was looking at her, color crept up her cheeks. She could feel it.

Frank nodded. "Must have been," he agreed. "Besides, you look better in pink than in white."

"Pink?"

Unable to resist, he ran just the tip of his finger along her cheek. Silky, like the petal of a rose that Mollie, his niece, would offer him from the meadow, he thought. "You're flushed."

"It's the heat."

A smile curved his lips. "You feel it, too?"

They weren't discussing the airport and they both knew it, but she had to cling to something. "Too many bodies in such a small space," she murmured.

He would have enjoyed getting her in a small space, he suddenly thought, but he felt it prudent not to voice his thoughts.

Instead, he nodded toward a lone vending machine that was standing guard against the wall. "Can I interest you in a candy bar while we're waiting?"

"No." She was against junk food in general, but then again, she hadn't eaten in a while and her stomach felt oddly hollow. Frank raised a brow, as if to prod her. It worked. "Oh, why not?"

"That's what I like. A decadent woman." He laughed, then gestured toward the candies displayed in the machine. "What's your pleasure?"

She shrugged, unable to choose. "I don't know. Surprise me."

Again the smile curved his lips and, this time straight into her soul. "All right, I will."

She felt as if she had just been issued a promise, and it didn't involve chocolate coating.

Donna swallowed hard.

"Hold my place," he cautioned, then nodded at the man and woman behind him. "I'll be right back." They looked at him and nodded stiffly.

When he returned, he had two large candy bars in his possession. Or, rather, one large one and another that he had already begun eating. Several passengers smiled at him, despite the fact that his clothes were splattered with blood.

The baby's birth had fostered a certain camaraderie between them.

He presented the wrapped bar to Donna. "There you are. A giant candy bar—for energy."

She nodded her thanks and tore off the paper, hungrier than she thought.

Frank glanced down at his clothing. "I guess I'm going to have to change my clothes before we land in Seattle. Otherwise, the police might want to pick me up for questioning."

He said it without any self-consciousness whatsoever. She caught herself wondering what sort of a man he was to be so self-assured, so comfortable with himself and others. "That was very impressive back there." Frank raised a quizzical brow at her statement. "Back in the airplane, with Rosemary."

He lifted his shoulder carelessly and then let it drop. "I didn't do anything. I was just there to receive the pass when it came. She did it all."

Modest, too. It was a nice added touch. She wondered if it was genuine. Howard Walker had been just as laid-back until she had turned him down when he asked her out. Then he had become belligerent.

"You kept her calm," she pointed out.

He grinned as he broke off a piece of chocolate. He and Mollie shared a common weakness when it came to chocolate. His niece had probably inherited it from him, he mused. "That was me I was trying to calm down. Rosemary just got in the way."

Donna studied him. "Don't take compliments easily, do you?"

Frank grinned. For just the slightest of seconds, a thought flashed through his mind. A scene. He and Donna on a soft bed, enjoying one another. He could feel his body responding even as the next second took the thought away. "Depends what kind."

Donna could feel the prick of tension shooting through her, traveling through her body. She lowered her eyes until all she was looking at was the candy bar.

The tension didn't go away. There was something here, shimmering between them in this tiny, overcrowded airport, something warm and inviting, and she had absolutely no idea what to do with it. She only knew that she hadn't experienced anything like this since Tony. He had been the only one to ever make her feel she was first and foremost a woman and everything else second. He could do it with a look.

The same kind of look that was in this man's eyes.

But Frank was a complete stranger to her, even if they'd shared some intimate moments together on the plane. She didn't even remember his last name.

Donna flinched, as if she could almost touch the feeling that was closing around her. Feelings. After all this time, *feelings*. They'd been in a deep freeze ever since she had found Tony's lifeless body that morning at the office. She had expected her emotions to remain that way forever. Frozen.

She would have preferred it that way.

Preoccupied, Donna hadn't realized that they'd inched their way up to one of the three telephones. She stared at it dumbly now, frantically grasping for the soothing numbness that had always existed within her. "Um, I think the telephone's free."

He thought he had seen panic flash in her eyes. Why? Was she that worried about her sons? Frank gestured to the public phone with the remainder of his candy bar. "Ladies first." He stepped back.

Donna was acutely aware of him as she threw in her change, even though he wasn't actually touching her.

He didn't have to.

Chapter Three

The din in the crammed airport settled to a minor rumble with occasional swells that were followed shortly thereafter by smaller rumbles. People were trying their best to get along in their common dilemma, but tempers were short. The fact that there was no coffee shop on the premises didn't help.

Donna tried to keep her call to Lisa brief, but first Taylor and then Stephen insisted on getting on and talking to her. When she hung up, the woman behind her glared as she snatched the receiver. Donna stepped aside just as Frank moved forward to the telephone next to her.

Hoping to avoid him for a while, Donna quietly dropped back.

The airport personnel had brought in a few folding chairs, but the effort fell pitifully short of its mark. Many of the travelers were forced to stand. Others sat around in clusters on the floor.

Donna found a spot by the bay window overlooking the runway to wait out the delay. As she sat down, pulling her legs in beneath her, Rafferty came hurrying over to her. He had a strange, bemused expression on his face.

Oh, God, don't let it be bad.

"It's the damnedest thing," he began before he had even managed to reach her.

Donna mentally crossed her fingers. "What?"

She started to rise, but he waved her back. There was no need for her to do anything. "Now the gauge is registering where it should be. I've got one of the airport mechanics looking at it to see what's wrong."

She didn't like instruments winking in and out like that. "What about the tanks themselves?"

"Fine. They're at the right level. No leaks, no anomalies." He spread his hands. It didn't make any sense. "I can't figure it out."

She wouldn't feel good about this until she had Walter look at the gauge. The mechanic she kept on salary had his odd quirks, but no one knew airplanes the way he did. "How long—?"

Rafferty shrugged. "The mechanic said half an hour. Maybe forty-five minutes."

An hour before they were airborne again, she judged, knowing how things managed to stretch out. "Fine. Let me know when we're ready."

He gave her a teasing salute and retreated to confer with the mechanic.

Donna glanced out the window and looked at her plane. *Her* plane. It did have a nice feel to it, she thought. Thank the Lord it was the gauge and nothing more serious, like a leak in one of the tanks. Still, it did seem rather odd. Donna sighed as she dragged a hand through her hair. There were too many things on her mind to wonder about a faulty gauge at the moment. Walter would get to the bottom of it when they landed.

When she turned back, there were a pair of well-worn brown cowboy boots standing next to her. Donna didn't have to look up to know that they belonged to Frank.

He was holding a paper container of coffee in each hand.

"Here, I thought you might like some." He handed her one, then sat down beside her.

"Oh, yes." Even vending-machine coffee had caffeine and, right now, she desperately needed it any way she could get it. Her energy level felt as if it were flagging. Donna swallowed and then closed her eyes, waiting for the kick to hit. "You're a lifesaver."

"I try." He settled back against the window. It wasn't comfortable, but the company, he mused, looking at her over his own cup, made up for it. "Any news?"

"You'll be happy to know that we'll be in the air within the hour." She took another long sip of her coffee. This time she could taste the paper-cup flavor, but it didn't matter. The brew was dark and it was warm and that was all that counted.

"Oh, I don't know about happy." Donna looked at him quizzically. No one liked being stranded. "I was going to use the downtime to get acquainted."

Though his words were innocent enough, something small and protective tensed within her. "I don't—"

He didn't give her a chance to back away. "Shy?" he guessed. "All right." He could give her some room. "I'll go first. My name is Frank Harrigan and I'm a nurse—" He said the words exactly as he had said them when he had addressed an assembly of fresh-faced children at Wilmington Falls Elementary School on career day.

The man was tall, handsome in a very rugged way and probably the least likely looking nurse she had ever seen. He'd told her he was a nurse before, but she hadn't had a chance to ask him about it. "Why a nurse?"

"Why not?" he countered easily. The coffee was bitter, but it was better than nothing, he supposed. "My sister had her heart set on being a doctor ever since she examined her first Barbie doll and pronounced said patient to have a ruptured appendix. I figured if she was going to work at the clinic, she'd need help."

The sunlight behind him was playing off his chiseled profile. The man, Donna caught herself thinking, could make money modeling as a superhero for the covers of comic books.

Donna blinked, forcing herself to focus on the conversation.

There was something too pat about his answer. "Why not become a doctor, too?"

Frank shrugged, crumpling his empty container in his hand. "I'm not too keen on performing surgery." He thought back across the years, not without a tinge of regret. Yet he had made his choice and was ultimately glad of it. It had worked out for the best. For all of them. "Besides, getting a degree as a nurse was faster, and we needed someone back at the old homestead."

Despite her desire to maintain distance between them, Donna was drawn in. She leaned forward, waiting for him to continue. "Meaning?"

She was asking for a little more than the *Reader's Digest* version. He held up a hand. "Let me take you back for a minute. My father was a doctor," he began, warming to the subject.

Donna couldn't help herself. A smile slipped across her lips. "Ah, the plot thickens."

Frank inclined his head in agreement. He was getting her out of that protective shell she'd erected around herself when they'd deplaned, he thought. Good.

"Exactly."

He felt an urge to slip his arm around her shoulders, the way he might with someone he was telling a story to. But he refrained, knowing that he would really be getting ahead of himself. It was just that he felt so comfortable with her, as if he had known her a long time. As if she had belonged in his life from the start.

It was an odd feeling, but he couldn't shake it any more than the very real, very strong attraction he felt toward her.

"My dad worked at one of the larger hospitals in San Francisco. By the time I'd reached my teens, he'd become fed up with city life." Frank snapped his fingers. "Suddenly, my family and I were whisked away to the land of Oz, otherwise known as Wilmington Falls."

He remembered how much he had hated living there at first, how much he had rebelled, threatening to run away and live with his friends. It was a wonder his mother's hair hadn't turned white then, instead of remaining the pale gold color it always was.

"For Jeannie, my younger sister, and me, it might as well have been Oz. Strictly a one-horse, backward town—or so we thought." Frank looked at Donna. He could tell that she was envisioning it all. He continued, thoroughly enjoying himself. "Anyway, it grew on us. My father was the only doctor for twenty miles in any direction. Jeannie wanted to be just like him. She went off to college to turn that dream into a reality." His voice lowered. "We were both away at school when he died." Even after all this time, Frank could feel a slight shiver pass over him at the memory. He still missed him. "I had to change my major quickly."

Donna had just raised the cup to her lips. She stopped, looking at him. "Change?"

Damn. He'd slipped. He hadn't meant to phrase it that way. Before his father had died, Frank had had all the intentions of becoming a doctor himself. He had even completed most of the premed requirements. But then Dr. Harrigan had passed away and suddenly choices had to be made. Choices and sacrifices. And there had been his mother to think of. Anne Harrigan was a strong woman, but without anyone to help her run it, the clinic would have closed. And it was the only medical clinic available in the small community. He couldn't turn his back on that.

Frank had quickly pleaded his case to the dean at his school. Through surprisingly kind understanding and a little sleight of hand, he had managed to have a great many of his existing credits transferred toward a degree in nursing. His training period amounted to hands-on experience that had almost succeeded in undoing him. He'd pulled double duty between the clinic in Wilmington Falls and the hospital located in the neighboring town until he was officially certified as an R.N.

During that period, when he'd slept in snatches and lost nearly twenty pounds, somehow, he and his mother had kept things going at the clinic until Jeannie had returned with her medical credentials. And Mollie.

But all that was a very private matter, something he didn't talk about. Something only his mother suspected. When she had asked him what had happened to his plans of becoming a doctor, he had shrugged carelessly and replied that he had changed his mind.

Frank's lips curved as he smiled at Donna. She was still waiting for an answer to her question.

"I was majoring in campus partying at the time." He figured she'd readily accept that. "I turned to something a little more practical, got my degree in nursing while helping out at the clinic and working at the hospital." He reeled off the rest of the story quickly. "My mother and I held down the fort until Jeannie returned. Lucky for me, she's a smart kid and got through her studies and residency in a record amount of time."

"Kid?" Donna thought it was an odd way to refer to someone with a medical degree. Was his sister a child prodigy? He certainly made her sound that way.

He laughed. "She's my little sister. To me, she'll always be a kid. Even when she's ninety." He inclined his head toward Donna and caught another faint whiff of her perfume. Sweet, clean and enticing. Just like her. "Jeannie likes that part of it."

The sound of his easy laugh coaxed her own laughter out. In fact, she thought bemusedly, he seemed to be coaxing a great deal out of her that she hadn't thought ready to be freed. Frank Harrigan, she realized, had a manner about him that seemed to bring all sorts of emotions swimming to the surface.

The late-afternoon light was dancing through her hair, bringing out reddish highlights amid the dark strands. He was tempted to close his hand around one and catch it as if it were a firefly.

His eyes met hers and he saw that there were still traces of reticence in them. He decided to give Donna a little push to get her started. "So why's a mother of two—two?" he asked as if he didn't already know.

Donna shifted. Her legs felt as if they were falling asleep beneath her. Frank's hand automatically shot out to steady her. She froze. There was something about his touch that went through all the layers, through politeness and distance, straight to the core.

A man touching a woman.

Donna could feel excitement rising within her and almost exhaled in relief when he withdrew his hand.

"Just two," she answered, struggling to keep her mind on the subject.

He shook his head. "I've got a niece and nephew, and there is no such thing as 'just' two kids. Two are like kinetic energy, bouncing off each other and you."

When she laughed and her smile reached her eyes, Frank knew he'd found the key to her self-imposed cell. He made himself more comfortable.

"Anyway, what's a mother of two doing flying all over the wide blue yonder?"

He assumed that she was a flight attendant, even though she didn't wear a uniform. The way she had taken charge on the plane indicated that she was, and she *had* identified herself as being with the airline. However, he found it odd. He had always envisioned flight attendants as unattached men and women who relished their freedom—not as parents who had school forms to fill out and bake sales to attend.

She sighed as she leaned back against the window. It had been a long, hard road, but she was making her way over it. The last of the outstanding hospital bills had been paid off at the beginning of the year. And the charter service was finally back in the black. She was even able to put aside a little money as a hedge against emergencies. Such as faulty fuel gauges, she thought with a smile.

"Paying for their food and a roof over their heads," she answered before she could think better of it. "Besides—" She smiled "—flying is all I know."

Frank's eyes swept over her with a deep, penetrating look that was sensual, seeming to delve into her innermost secrets. Secrets she didn't want to share. "I sincerely doubt that."

Donna looked down into her empty coffee container, trying hard not to react to this man. She was losing. "I was flying one of these planes before I was even out of my teens. My father insisted on it. Said it would help me understand the business."

"Flying the plane?" Frank repeated. He considered himself to be very modern, but envisioning her behind the controls did take him aback. "Wait a minute, I think I missed something. You're not the flight attendant?"

She laughed as she shook her head. That might have been an easier life than the one she had chosen for herself, she thought. Someone else could worry about the problems then. "No, Windsong doesn't have any. But maybe someday we will."

Which led him to the question he had about the second half of her statement. "We? Is that a figurative 'we' or a possessive 'we'?"

She smiled. "Possessive. Very possessive."

"You own it?"

She laughed shortly. "No, the bank does. It lets me play with it and spend long hours staring at computer screens, trying to find a way to balance my tallies and pay everyone. But my name's on the deed, if that's what you're asking." She sighed, thinking of one long phone call she'd had just the other week. "I'm the one you come to with complaints."

"I can't think of any." Knowing he was moving fast, he still plunged ahead. "Was your husband a pilot?"

She shook her head. "No, he took over management of the business after my father died," she said, her voice stoic. *That was when all the trouble began.* "It was just a little beyond him."

The next moment she silently upbraided herself. Why was she admitting something like that to a stranger?

It was a happy marriage, he decided with a touch of envy. She was still grieving. He couldn't help wondering what it felt like to have someone love him that much. Or to love someone that much. He hadn't been lucky that way.

Yet.

"How long were you married?" Her head jerked up and she slanted a look at him. He'd hit a nerve, he thought. "If you don't mind my asking."

She was being unduly skittish, she thought. Donna forced herself to relax. He was only making conversation, and it was time, as Lisa had told her, to let go. At least a little.

"I don't mind you asking, and the answer is not long enough." Pressing her lips together, she turned the plain gold band around on her finger, as if twisting it could somehow turn time back, or make it stop altogether. But wishes like that were for children, and she wasn't a child. She looked up at Frank. "Anyway, after Tony died, I took over. It was either that, or face the possibility of declaring bankruptcy. I wasn't about to do that, so I went to work. We all have to eat."

"Nasty habit." Frank glanced toward the vending machine. "Speaking of which, want another candy bar?"

"No." One was enough to make her feel guilty. She was always lecturing her sons about how candy was really bad for them.

Though he was a nurse, he was a closet junk food junkie. "Potato chips?"

She laughed and she shook her head. "No. I think we'll be out of here before we starve to death, Mr. Harrigan. I can hold out for a decent meal."

One that he'd like to take her to, he thought. But a few things had to be ironed out first. "No one calls me Mr. Harrigan. I think after what we've been through, you can definitely call me Frank, Donna."

The sound of her name on his tongue caused a warmth to permeate within her, like a cup of hot coffee winding its way through her body on a chilly morning at the airfield.

She was having a completely adolescent reaction, Donna chided herself. But then, she thought, other than Tony, there had never been any other man in her life. By modern standards, she judged that put her way behind the average woman as far as romances went. If anything, it placed her somewhere around the delightful emotional age of a sixteen-year-old savoring the very first buds of infatuation.

A very young sixteen-year-old, she thought, cataloguing her limited experience. Her next thought was of the funeral and the dark mantle that had fallen on her shoulders that day.

A *very* young sixteen, she amended, and yet a very old one, too.

They continued talking for a while longer. Bit by bit, Frank managed to draw her out a little more. He liked the way her eyes sparkled when she talked about her sons. When he thought about it, Frank realized that there wasn't a single thing he *didn't* like about her. And he'd never met anyone quite like her before.

As far as he was concerned, he could have spent the remainder of his vacation right here, on the floor of the crowded airport, talking to this woman.

But then he saw the pilot approaching them. "Ready to roll anytime you are, boss lady."

"Great. Have them make the announcement that we're loading." Donna breathed a sigh of relief as Rafferty went to find someone in charge of the loudspeaker. She rose, testing her legs. When Frank got up next to her, the space between them seemed to somehow shrink until there was no room for her to move.

The air in her lungs evaporated.

Their eyes met and held for a long moment.

For just a second, she thought he was going to kiss her—and the idea was as exciting as it was frightening.

The announcement came over the broadcast system at that moment. Rafferty's resonant voice told them that the plane was ready to depart. The words were drowned out by cheers.

Frank inclined his face to Donna's in order to be heard. "Just in time," he told her. "The change machine is out of change and the vending machine is almost out of selections."

"Things always have a way of working out," she assured him as she walked out of the terminal.

Watching her as she walked away, he was inclined to agree.

Coming to, Frank hurried to keep up with her. She wasn't going to get away that easily. He felt as if he were suddenly chasing after Cinderella at the stroke of midnight. He knew he wanted another chance to dance with her before she left the ball.

Frank placed a hand on her shoulder to anchor her for a moment as they reached the boarding area. "Are you busy tonight? I'm visiting a friend in Seattle, but I'm sure he'd understand if—"

"No."

The single word snapped out of her mouth like an arrow released in flight. For a few minutes back in the terminal, because he was so gregarious, she'd forgotten herself and opened up more than she should have. But there had been something humming between them, something she didn't want beginning again. Donna had absolutely no desire to reopen old wounds by enjoying the company of a man who made her feel like a woman again.

No desire at all.

Desire.

The word rose up and shimmered before her like heat rising from the asphalt on a scorching summer's day.

Donna could feel his eyes on her, his brows drawn together quizzically. He didn't deserve to be snapped at, not after the way he had helped her. Not after the way he had risen to the emergency and delivered Rosemary's baby. But she didn't want to go into the reasons she was so leery of relationships that held the least hint of being more than casual.

And there was more than a possibility of that with him. She could *feel* it.

Donna moistened her lips. "I mean, Taylor's sick and I want to spend some time with him—"

The thought of a cozy evening at her home sounded good to him. He'd gotten corny in his old age, he decided. The idea of hearth and home was beginning to have a lot of appeal.

"That's fine," Frank said easily. "I can come along and offer you the benefit of my vast medical experience—free of charge."

She wasn't the type to run, had never been, and it went against her grain now. But she had to. If she didn't take that first step, she wouldn't have to worry about the last one.

"Thank you, but no," Donna said firmly. Her voice took on a formal edge. "Now, if you'll excuse me, I have work to do." The smile on her face was entirely impersonal. Turning away, she hurried toward the plane.

Frank stepped back. He shoved his hands into his pockets, wondering what had gone wrong. A moment ago, they had been getting along just fine. He knew he'd been making headway. And then she had suddenly shored up her beaches, as if he were the attacking enemy.

Was it something he'd said?

There were no further opportunities for Frank to talk to her. Donna made sure of it. During the remainder of the flight, she stayed in the cockpit. Since there was no copilot on this flight, Donna sat in the vacant seat and completed the trip there. She took over the controls on the last leg of the flight. Flying always managed to soothe her.

Before she knew it, it was time to land. Home, she thought with relief.

"Another almost perfect run," she murmured, unbuckling her seat belt.

"I'd have O'Connell take a look at this gauge if I were you," Rafferty advised. "I didn't have a whole lot of confidence in that mechanic they had back there." He jerked a thumb in the general direction of their flight pattern.

"Way ahead of you," she agreed.

He rose, but Donna remained seated. "Aren't you coming?"

"In a minute." She wanted to be sure that Frank had deplaned before she walked out of the cockpit.

Rafferty picked up his small flight bag. "Wouldn't mind having you as my permanent copilot."

She laughed. "You're just lazy."

"Yeah." A smile crept along his lips. "There's that, too." Adjusting his hat rakishly over one eye, Rafferty left.

When Donna finally emerged from the cockpit, Frank's seat was empty and he was gone.

Good.

Donna's sigh of relief was mingled with just the slightest hint of disappointment as she collected her carry-on luggage. The next moment, she was pushing the emotion away. She wasn't disappointed. She was glad.

Well, maybe not so glad, she amended as she got off the plane and unconsciously scanned the immediate area. He wasn't anywhere to be seen.

But nonetheless, she silently insisted, she was relieved. If relief had an odd texture to it, creating a lump that sat heavily in her chest, that was just an aberration. Yes, there had been an attraction, but that was just the trouble. She had no intentions of being attracted to a man—ever. Once was enough to lose her heart and then have it broken.

Donna stopped by her office to talk to Walter about the whimsical fuel gauge. As he went to acquaint himself with the problem, Donna contemplated the mounting pile of paperwork on her desk, but her heart wasn't in it. There was Monday for that. The bills didn't have to be faced for another three weeks.

She hurried outside. Seattle weather drizzled down at her, wet and warm this last week in May. Lucky thing she liked curly hair, she thought, feeling hers curl about her head as she skirted around a couple who were struggling with their luggage.

Donna walked directly through the crowded parking lot toward her car. She always parked in the exact same location, so she wouldn't have trouble finding her car.

Her thoughts tumbled over each other and somehow managed to find their way back to Frank.

It would never have worked out, she reflected doggedly. There was distance to take into consideration. He wasn't from around here. What sort of future could they have had with him in Wilmington Falls—wherever that was—and her here?

God, just listen to her. She'd been giving them a relation-ship and they hadn't even been in each other's company for more than a few hours!

A very long and pregnant few hours, she amended. As for a relationship... well, that *might* have been something she could have explored more leisurely if she had agreed to his invitation....

No, no exploring, she told herself firmly, unlocking the car door. She tossed in her bag and then sat down behind the wheel. Larger, angrier drops hit the windshield as she sat, staring out. No exploring, no reopening, no nothing.

Donna turned on the ignition. She was fine just the way she was, with her hectic life and her more hectic kids.

Fine. Just fine.

Squaring her shoulders, she guided the car into the stream of light early-evening traffic.

He certainly hadn't tried very hard, she thought as she took the turn that led to her modest one-story house. Which was just as well, she argued back. The man had made her pulse jump, for heaven's sake, and there was no room in her life any longer for things like that, she thought with a bit-tersweet pang. The only reason he was in her mind at all was because it *had* been such a long time for her. It was a little like turning on the radio as the last strains of a wonderful song died away and realizing that perhaps, just perhaps, you wanted to hear the whole song just one more time.

She had had her song, Donna reminded herself. And it had ended in a funeral dirge. She had placed all her love, all her dreams, into Anthony McCullough. And he had died. Willingly. He had committed suicide when the business kept going downhill, unable to stand the guilt. As if she could have blamed him.

What she could blame him for, she thought, the hurt welling up again, thick and hot within her chest, was for leaving her. For leaving the boys.

She forced herself to focus on the present as she brought her '85 Mustang to a stop inside the garage that was crammed with forgotten toys and Lisa's newer car. There was no use in rehashing the past. It was over, and she had her sons to think of.

Lisa had left the door open for her, she thought with relief. Bless that woman.

Getting out, Donna suddenly felt bone tired. But she was happy. She was home.

The moment she opened the door leading from the garage into the house, Donna was assailed by shouts. Taylor and Stephen came running toward her. It was as if both of her sons had been waiting by the door for the sound of her return.

"Mom!" Taylor cried as he gave her a hug. "You're home!"

His unexpected enthusiasm surprised her. Taylor was at the point where he was struggling between being a little boy and being a worldly preteen.

She draped an arm around each boy. Nothing could be better than this, Donna thought happily. Nothing. "Of course I'm home. Where else would I be but with my two handsome men?"

Stephen said nothing. He wrapped his arms around his mother's waist and buried his face in her hip, holding on for all he was worth.

Donna thought she felt his small shoulder shaking. "Stephen, what's wrong, honey?"

Lisa entered from the family room just behind the boys. Donna raised her eyes quizzically to her, but Lisa only shook her head. She didn't know what was going on any more than Donna did.

Taylor had his own explanation for it. "Oh, he's just a crybaby, aren't you, Step-On?" He laughed as he gave his brother a shove.

Donna frowned. "Taylor, you know I don't like you calling him that." Disengaging Stephen's hold, Donna bent down and looked into his face. His cheeks were damp. She cupped his chin in her hand. "Now, what's this all about, sweetheart?"

Stephen sniffed. "I thought you weren't coming back anymore."

She hugged him to her, holding him against her heart. "Oh, Stevie, of course I was coming back." She looked down at him. "Don't I always?"

He nodded, then hiccuped before answering. "But Aunt Lisa said the plane was having trouble."

Donna knew what it had to be like for him, being so young and with only one parent. It had to be frightening. She gave Stephen her most reassuring smile. "Nothing big, pumpkin. Just think of it as a little car trouble."

Stephen screwed up his face, trying to do as she said. It didn't work. "But the car can't fall down when it has trouble."

She rose. Sometimes Stephen was too smart for his own good. "Good point. But you know that I've told you airplanes have a lot less accidents than cars do. And anyway, I don't really fly all that much anymore." She cupped his chin in her hand again and gave it an affectionate squeeze. "Better?"

The small boy scrubbed his face with his hands. "Better."

Well, that was settled. She looked at her older son. The last time she'd seen him, he'd had tissues in both hands. "Taylor, how's your cold?"

"What cold?" he crowed. "I wasted it."

"That's my guy." Donna turned toward her sister-in-law. "Anything new to report?"

The blond woman saluted. "No Indians attacking, no rebellions on the home front, Captain. The fort is as you left it."

Donna laughed. "That's the last time I buy you a tape of *The Last of the Mohicans* video." She stretched and rotated her shoulders. It had been a long, long day. All of it, she thought, remembering Frank.

But just as she was savoring the peace, both boys began talking at once, vying for her attention. Their voice levels grew and swelled as each tried to outshout the other.

Donna whistled—loud—and held up a hand as if she were a soccer referee, calling time. When she finally got it, she said, "I'm going to change out of these clothes and then you can all fill me in on what's been going on. One at a time,'' she cautioned.

She looked from one eager face to the other. It was as if they'd split the children between them, she and Tony. Stephen took after her side of the family and Taylor, with his wheat-colored hair and soft brown eyes, could just as easily have been mistaken for Lisa's son rather than hers. "That sound fair?''

"Fair," Stephen responded.

Taylor looked at her cagily. "Will you listen to me first?''

Definitely Tony's side of the family. Tony had always pushed for the edge, always wanting to win. Donna laughed, then glanced over her shoulder at Lisa. "Have them draw straws, Lisa.''

Smiling, she went off to her bedroom.

As Donna passed the threshold, she thought of the storm and what could have been. She ran her fingers along the doorjamb, savoring the feel.

God, but it felt good to be home.

Chapter Four

The sound of sour chords being strummed with more determination than dexterity vibrated in the air as Donna returned to the family room. Taylor was sitting on the sofa, his face screwed up in complete concentration as he hunched over his father's old guitar, struggling to produce something recognizable on it.

He was failing miserably.

Stephen was hanging on to the arm of the sofa, rocking on his toes. His expression was smug. "You'll never learn to play it in time," he jeered, still smarting from Taylor's taunt that he was a baby.

"I will, too, Step-On." Temper mounting, Taylor looked as if he would rather have used the guitar as a weapon than a musical instrument.

Donna saw that Lisa was taking the exchange in stride. Apparently this had been going on for the past two days. Employing restraint, Donna refrained from admonishing Taylor for distorting his brother's name again. She tried not to flinch as another fractured chord corkscrewed its way through the air.

"In time for what, Taylor?"

Taylor's head jerked up. The sheepish smile came and went in the blink of an eye. It was replaced by a defensive look that dared her to talk him out of it. "The talent contest."

Inwardly, Donna winced. He'd be laughed off the stage. But she knew there was no talking him out of it. Just as his father had been, Taylor was stubborn. Any criticism, any suggestion, she might offer about perhaps waiting another year would only make him that much more determined to participate in this year's contest. She couldn't be the one to squelch his aspirations. For a moment she wished that Robert Preston's method in *The Music Man* worked. If she remembered correctly, he had instructed the children to think the music through their instruments. And through the magic of Hollywood, it had happened.

But this wasn't Hollywood.

Tony had promised to teach Taylor how to play his beloved guitar, but he had never gotten around to it.

Donna sighed and blotted out the memory. She mustered an encouraging smile. "When is the talent show?"

Taylor hit another chord. He raised his chin defiantly. "Two weeks."

Lisa was clearing off the dining room table. Mail, homework and crayons were scattered all over it. She paused to exchange looks with Donna. Unless a miracle occurred, two weeks would not be enough time for Taylor to master even the simplest song.

Lisa shook her head. "Don't look at me," she told Donna. "I don't know how to play. Tony was the musical one in the family, not me."

Donna licked her lips, searching for the best way to say this. She placed her hand on her son's shoulder and felt it stiffen, as if he were fending away her remark before she even made it. "Taylor, maybe you should try something else for the talent contest."

Taylor shook his head, his fingers gripping the neck of the guitar tightly. He scowled as he looked at it. He really wanted to play. Why wasn't it easier? He raised his eyes to his mother, expecting her to understand. "I can't sing, I can't dance and I can't do any magic tricks—"

"You can't play the guitar, either," Stephen piped up. He danced back out of reach before Taylor could take a swing at him.

Donna gave the younger boy a warning look. "Stephen, that's enough. He can't get anywhere if he doesn't try." In this case, she didn't think he would get anywhere if he *did* try, at least not in two weeks, but she kept that observation to herself.

She studied Taylor for a moment. He had taken Tony's death the hardest. Could his wanting to play the guitar at the talent show be his way of feeling closer to his father?

Donna perched on the edge of the sofa's arm. "Why is it so important for you to be in the talent contest, honey?" she asked softly.

Taylor's expression didn't change. Anger at the guitar and determination still creased his brow. "Because Chris, Jason and Pete are in it."

Donna tried to match the names to a significant piece of information in her mind. "Aren't those the boys you told me pick on you?"

"Yeah." He spat the word out. "I want to kick their butts."

Well, that wasn't a phrase he'd learned from her, but Donna knew it could have been worse. She tactfully chose not to comment on it. "And you want to use a guitar to do it."

This time his eyes lit up when he said, "Yeah." He could remember sitting at his father's feet, listening, entranced, as magical sounds emerged out of the instrument he was holding. Sounds Taylor was determined to duplicate.

Donna thought that Taylor would have a better chance "kicking butt" if he gripped the guitar like a bat and used it that way, but she bit her tongue. She couldn't help him herself, but she could at least find that help for him.

"All right." She smiled at him and was rewarded with a smile in return. They were back on the same side again. "Maybe we can get you some guitar lessons. Quick." She winked and Taylor laughed. The tension left his shoulders and they no longer looked as if a coat hanger were embedded in them. "Get me the Yellow Pages." It was rather late to reach someone tonight, but at least she could find a number to call in the morning.

Taylor jumped to his feet, the guitar's neck still clutched in his hand. Standing on his toes, he brushed her cheek with a kiss. "You're super, Mom."

She sighed, thinking that Taylor's learning enough to "wow" his enemies at the contest was probably hopeless, but that she wasn't going to be the one to break his bubble. And who knew? Maybe miracles *did* happen.

"I do my best."

"I'll get the phone book," Stephen sang out, dancing off on his toes. He was mimicking Taylor, whom, in more peaceful moments, he actually idolized.

The guitar was temporarily abandoned on the sofa as Taylor raced off after his brother. "She asked *me* to get it, Dork."

Never a dull moment. Donna looked at Lisa. "Think making them sit still for an 'Ozzie and Harriet' marathon would get them to act differently toward each other? David and Ricky never behaved this way."

Lisa laughed. Stephen and Taylor's attitude toward each other wasn't all that different from the way she and Tony had treated one another some fifteen years ago. Gathering the last of the magazines from the table, she tucked them under her arm. "Not a chance. Besides, you never got a chance to see the way David and Ricky behaved *off* camera."

"I suppose you're right." Donna nodded, resigned to enduring warfare for several more years.

The doorbell rang just as the boys tumbled back into the room. Taylor was balancing the thick telephone book on top of his head, his hands raised and ready on either side of it in case it slipped. Stephen was leaping up and down, trying to reach the book in order to knock it down.

"Quit it, Step-On," Taylor snarled.

"I'll get it," Lisa volunteered, glad to duck out of the war zone for a moment.

"If it's a door-to-door salesman, ask him if I can run away with him," Donna called after Lisa.

She turned to look at her squabbling sons. Some days, their arguing was harder to endure than others, but after being in a lurching airplane, it seemed like a piece of cake. A piece of cake she bit into gladly.

"Taylor," she began as sternly as she could, which under the circumstances wasn't very, "you don't like those boys at school because they pick on you, right?"

"Right." He handed her the Yellow Pages and then picked up his guitar again as if it were an enchanted sword that he could use to beat his enemies. "They wouldn't if I was bigger—"

He was on the wrong track and would barrel away in a moment if she didn't stop him. Bracing the heavy book against her chest with one hand, she placed the other on Taylor's shoulder and looked into his eyes. "That's not the point I'm getting at. If you don't like the way they treat you, why do you treat Stephen the same way?"

Taylor's mouth fell open and his eyes widened in protest. "I don't."

"Yes, you do," Stephen chimed in, careful to keep their mother between them.

"Shut up, Step-On...." As soon as the words were out of his mouth, Taylor looked up guiltily at his mother. "I guess I do, huh?" he mumbled.

She smiled, already softening. She remembered the impatience of childhood too well to remain annoyed for more than a few minutes. "What do you think?"

Thin shoulders rose and fell carelessly. "I think I shouldn't treat him like the dork he is."

Donna shook her head, stifling a laugh for Stephen's benefit. "It's a start." She flipped open the ponderous book. "Now let's see if we can find you a kindly guitar teacher who makes house calls and doesn't charge much money—and maybe occasionally performs a miracle or two on the side."

A deep, masculine voice behind Donna said, "I don't think you have to look very far."

Donna dropped the telephone book. It fell, its yellow pages splaying at her feet like a monarch butterfly taking a curtain call.

No, it couldn't be.

Could it?

Donna turned around very slowly, then stared, dumbfounded. Frank, his suitcase in his hand, was standing next to Lisa in the doorway.

Frank saw the way Donna was looking at his suitcase. "Don't worry." The smile was as guileless, as easy, as it had been at the airport. "I'm not moving in. I'm just here for a little advice." He set the suitcase down by the sofa, out of the way.

Her sons were staring and Donna could literally see the questions multiplying in Lisa's head. But for now, everyone was quiet. Listening.

"Do you always look for advice with your suitcase in your hand?"

He was here. He was actually here. She couldn't believe it. She'd been utterly certain she would never see him again.

Donna tried to still the wild, completely uncalled-for fluttering she felt in her stomach.

He'd had no choice but to bring the suitcase with him, Frank thought. There had been no place to leave it. "I do if I don't have a place to stay."

Just how unorthodox and impulsive was this man? Donna shook her head as if trying to absorb what he was telling her. "Let me get this straight. You flew to Seattle and *didn't* make a hotel reservation?"

He noticed that she had taken a step back toward her children. She probably thought he was crazy. Maybe he was, just a little, he mused, looking at her. Otherwise, why was he here, standing in her family room?

"There was no reason to. I was going to be staying with a friend."

"But?" she asked suspiciously.

Frank shrugged, still mystified by it himself. "He was called away on business."

Donna's brow rose. Her expression told Frank that she thought he was making the whole thing up. He had to admit that it certainly sounded weird to him. Greg hadn't been at the airport to meet him as prearranged. Thinking something had undoubtedly come up, Frank had taken a cab to Greg's apartment, but there had been no answer when he knocked. The landlady had walked by just at the right moment, however, and had informed him that Greg had left a message with her for Frank. An emergency situation had arisen that morning and Greg had had to fly to Japan on business. Greg had no idea how long he'd be gone. There had been no mention of Frank staying at Greg's apartment in the interim, so Frank had left.

Donna glanced at the suitcase by the sofa. Was he going to ask her to put him up? Unconsciously, she straightened, bracing her shoulders.

Frank pretended he didn't notice. "I know it sounds strange, but it is the truth. And since I don't know the area..." He trailed off, feeling himself on very shaky ground. She was looking at him as if trying to decide whether he was an ax murderer who was trying to get her to trust him. "I was wondering if you could recommend a good hotel around here."

Donna looked down at the splayed phone book at her feet. She supposed it was a legitimate request. "I think I can help you out there."

She bent down for the book, but Frank was faster. He handed the telephone directory to her, his eyes smiling into hers.

Donna felt her breath growing short again.

"Who *is* he, Mom?" Taylor demanded, wheat-colored brows knitting together in sharp suspicion. Stephen had shrunk back, waiting first to see what his mother and his brother would do and say.

She didn't like Taylor's unfriendly tone. She hadn't raised him to be disrespectful. But lately, Taylor had become more than a handful. She supposed he needed a man's firm hand to guide him. His father's hand. Too bad, she thought defensively, all there was was her.

"He's—"

Frank stepped forward and held out his hand to the boy. "Frank Harrigan. Your mother and I met on the flight coming to Seattle today."

Taylor merely looked at Frank's outstretched hand. His suspicions multiplied across his young face as he took a protective stand by his mother, the young prince guarding the queen from the evil black knight. Frank remembered having similar feelings about his mother during one of his father's absences.

Donna had no such memories to fall back on. "Taylor, where are your manners?"

Because his brother didn't seem to like the man, Stephen stepped forward and literally shoved his small hand into Frank's. He was all smiles. "Hi, I'm Stephen."

The boy looked like a miniature of Donna, Frank thought. "Pleased to meet you, Stephen. Your mom told me a lot about you boys."

The scowl deepened on Taylor's face. "Why?" he wanted to know.

Enough was enough. "Taylor," Donna began sharply.

Frank raised a hand to stop her admonishment before it had a chance to unfurl.

"That's okay," he assured her easily, looking at Taylor. "It's up to the man of the family to check out strangers. You can't be too cautious these days."

Well, they were in agreement there, Donna thought. Particularly about strangers who came to your house with disarming manners and suitcases.

"Yes, I know. You never know what might follow you home." She looked at him pointedly.

Frank laughed. "Oh, but I didn't follow you home. I went to my friend's apartment first, remember?"

Donna flushed, knowing that she had made it sound as if she thought herself irresistible to him. The next heartbeat, however, brought another suspicion. "Then how did you know where I lived?"

His face was the picture of innocence. "I asked the pilot a couple of questions about you, about Windsong Airlines, really. I figured you didn't live that far from the airport and I looked you up in the telephone book. The rest is history."

If he could look her up, why couldn't he have looked up a hotel while he was at it? she wondered.

"Mom, weren't you going to find that music teacher for me?" Taylor prompted impatiently. His eyes indicated the Yellow Pages she was again clutching to her chest.

This was where he had come in, Frank thought. "Guitar lessons?" he guessed as he picked up the instrument from the sofa.

Taylor made a lunge for the guitar. "Hey, that's my dad's." He might as well have shouted, "Hands off!"

"I won't hurt it." Frank shifted his eyes to the boy's face and somehow Taylor's hot protest was temporarily quelled. Instead, he watched as Frank sat down and began to strum it.

Donna watched his fingers caressing the strings. He played as if he were making love to the instrument. She had to struggle to keep the shiver that jumped along her spine under control. Frank raised his eyes once and smiled at her, as if he knew what she was thinking. As if he were playing her instead of the instrument in his hands.

Sweet, throbbing music filled the air as he played a ballad. "I learned to play on a guitar just like this one," he told Taylor.

Stephen was already a convert. He planted himself down next to Frank on the sofa. "You play a lot?"

The music began to swell as Frank played a riff from a song that seemed to flow into his fingertips. "Whenever I get a chance." Because the sensual ballad was getting to him, he switched tunes, picking up an old rock-and-roll song in the middle.

Lisa had stood on the sidelines, quietly observing the scene. The beat had her tapping her foot in time. He played well, really well. Her sister-in-law was clearly impressed, Donna noted with a tinge of growing exasperation.

"When I was in high school, I put together my own band. We still get together when we can, just to jam."

That won Taylor over. The older boy sat down next to Frank, awe written as clearly across his face as if it had been scrawled there with a Magic Marker. He forgot to be suspicious and belligerent. Frank was now in danger of being elevated, at least temporarily, to the status of hero. "You do? A real band?"

Frank smiled inwardly, surprised at the warm sensation spreading inside him. He hadn't expected to feel this good about Taylor's reaction. "Yes, a real band."

"Get many gigs?" Taylor had recently learned the word and now rolled it importantly around on his tongue.

"Now and again," Frank conceded, continuing to play. "We play on weekends so that it doesn't interfere with our jobs."

Stephen stared, fascinated as Frank's fingers moved quickly along the strings. "What do you do?"

"Mr. Harrigan's a nurse," Donna said. She saw that her answer caught everyone by surprise, including Lisa. Her sons gaped first at her, then at Frank, who smiled to himself at the boys' reaction. It was evident that they didn't believe their mother.

"A nurse?" Stephen echoed, scratching his head exaggeratedly as little boys do when they are puzzled.

"*Girls* are nurses." Taylor almost sneered the pronouncement.

Frank changed tunes again, working up a single-handed rendition of "Dueling Banjos."

"Not anymore. Men and women can be anything they want to be, as long as they have the ability. Look at your mom—she's a pilot." His relaxed tone was in direct contrast to the frantic throbbing of his music. He ended with a flair, then handed the guitar back to Taylor. "It's just a matter of determination." His eyes held the boy's and he saw a tiny piece of himself there, as he had been once. "Do you want to play the guitar?"

"Yeah." Taylor's voice fairly pulsed with enthusiasm. He wanted to play like his dad, like Frank. "Can you teach me?"

Frank looked up at Donna, knowing that he had overstepped himself. "May I?"

"Yeah, may he, Mom?" Taylor asked, eager. "Pleease?" he said, stretching out the one-syllable word.

"He's good, Mom," Stephen said. "And Taylor needs help real bad."

For once, Taylor didn't contradict his brother.

Donna sighed and shook her head. She was definitely outnumbered here. She debated a moment and decided that there would be no harm in it. And if he could help Taylor, so much the better. After all, it was only temporary.

"Well," she began guardedly. Her sons were already jumping up and down. "If you don't have anything else to do—"

Frank spread his hands wide. "Not at the moment."

"What about finding a hotel room?" she said quietly, her wariness returning. "Or were you planning on going back home to Wilbur Falls?"

"Wilmington," he corrected easily. "And I've decided to hang around for a while." Taylor was eagerly shoving the guitar back into his hands. "You can always give me the name of a hotel later."

As long as it wasn't too much later, Donna thought. Giving up, she gestured toward Taylor. "He's all yours, then."

Withdrawing into the kitchen, Donna was aware that Lisa was only half a step behind her. Half a step and curious as hell. Acting nonchalant, Donna opened the refrigerator and took out a bag of carrots, then took down the decorative cutting board from where it hung on the wall.

Lisa watched as Donna quickly scrubbed the skins off five carrots. "What are you doing?"

With a long knife poised over the row of neatly lined carrots, Donna began to chop. "I'm cutting carrots."

That wasn't what she was referring to. Lisa waved an impatient hand toward the family room. "A gorgeous man shows up on your doorstep and you're in the kitchen cutting carrots?"

Donna spared Lisa a glance before continuing with her work. "I have to. Today's Angelina's day off and the carrots haven't learned how to cut themselves."

Exasperated, Lisa placed her hand over the knife's black hilt. "Who *is* he?"

Donna raised her eyes, her hand still. "I would have thought you'd have asked that question at the door before letting him in."

Donna was being evasive, Lisa thought. She'd seen a certain look enter her sister-in-law's eyes when she'd walked into the room with Frank. The same kind of look she had seen on Donna's face when Donna had been with Tony, so Lisa wasn't about to let this go. "He said he was looking for you. I thought he was a friend of yours."

Donna frowned. Though she was very friendly, *friend* was not a term she bandied about loosely. The word *friend* indicated a bond that took time to forge. "I've known him—" she glanced at her watch "—for a little less than half a day."

Lisa's mouth curved as she peeked into the family room and saw Frank with Taylor. "I'd certainly like to get to know him a lot longer than that."

Done, Donna deposited the carrots into a pot and added water before setting the pot on the stove. "Go ahead. You have my blessings."

"I don't have his and that's the important thing," Lisa said honestly. When Donna looked at her sharply, Lisa continued. "When he walked in, he looked at you as if you were a mound of French vanilla ice cream and he was the hot chocolate sauce."

Donna refused to let the image get to her. Instead, she opened the refrigerator, looking for the open jar of spaghetti sauce she had shoved in there two days ago. "You're on a diet again, aren't you?"

It was a safe guess. It seemed as if—three weeks out of the month—Lisa was experimenting with a new diet, though she certainly didn't look as if she needed one. "Yes, but my diet has nothing to do with it. You're changing the subject."

Donna tried again. "There *is* no subject, Lisa." Locating the jar, she took it out and slammed the refrigerator door a little harder than she meant to. "He was on the flight. I met him when another passenger went into labor and—"

"Whoa." Lisa held up both hands, overwhelmed. "Back up here. Someone went into labor?"

But Donna just shook her head. She didn't feel like going into the details now. "It's a long story. Maybe I'll tell you tomorrow."

The sauce found its way into a second pot. She accepted a third from Lisa. A large one big enough to cook spaghetti. Donna always liked spaghetti dinners when she returned from a trip.

"Right now, I—" She stopped as Stephen came running into the room. "Yes, Stephen?"

"Can Frank stay for dinner, Mom?" He tugged on her arm as if that would make her agree.

Manners didn't last long these days, she thought helplessly. Still, she had to try. "What happened to 'Mr. Harrigan'?"

Stephen shook his head as he laughed at his mother's forgetfulness. "That's Frank, Mommy," he reminded her. "Can he? Huh, can he? The dining room's all clean and everything."

This was getting out of hand. The man was getting entrenched in her family far too quickly for her liking. "I really don't think he should—"

"Yes." Lisa firmly overruled Donna. Stephen skipped off as Donna looked at her sister-in-law sharply. "The man has nowhere to stay and he probably hasn't eaten yet," Lisa said in defense of her decision. "Where's your sense of charity, Donna?"

Her defenses on alert, Donna took out a box of spaghetti and pried open one end. Her nail chipped. "You're making me sound like Scrooge."

Lisa took the box from her and shook out the long strands onto a paper towel. "More like a hiding vestal virgin."

Donna narrowed her brows. "Vestal virgins don't have two sons," she pointed out.

Lisa waited for the water to start boiling. "Then stop behaving like one," she counseled easily. "He's obviously interested. Otherwise he would have asked a cabdriver to take him to the nearest hotel instead of showing up here."

Donna had already thought of that. "Yes, I know. That's what I'm afraid of."

The water in the pot was boiling. Lisa tossed in the spaghetti and then took Donna's hands in hers. "Stop fluttering about the kitchen like a moving target for a minute and listen to me."

"First I'm a vestal virgin, then I'm a moving target. Make up your mind, Lisa." But Donna remained standing where she was.

Lisa sensed what the other woman was going through. Over the past two years, she had come to love Donna very much and she wanted to see her happy.

"Tony was a great guy. I loved him dearly. And I miss him very much, too. But he's gone and you're not. It's time to get on with your life."

Lisa wasn't saying anything she hadn't said before. But this time, there was someone sitting in the next room who might make a difference. Lisa didn't want to see Donna throwing that possibility away.

"I *am* getting on." Donna drew her hands away, then dragged one through her hair. "I'm getting on with it so much, I'm exhausted."

Lisa shook her head. "I don't mean work and the boys. I mean your life as a woman."

Donna grabbed hold of a spatula and raised it as if preparing to duel with Lisa's words. "A woman is not defined by the relationship she has with a man."

"No," Lisa readily agreed, and then smiled. "But it certainly makes life a hell of a lot more interesting." Lisa played her ace card as she looked at Donna knowingly. "The color rose in your face the minute you looked at him."

Donna shrugged as she began to stir the pasta. "That was shock."

It was a lot more than that and they both knew it. And one of them, Lisa judged, was afraid of it.

She opened her mouth to contradict Donna, then stopped and cocked her head.

"Listen." When Donna looked at her, puzzled, Lisa nodded toward the family room.

Donna dried her hands on a towel and moved closer to the doorway. Very hesitant, slow strains were emerging from the other room. The notes were choppy, but they were definitely notes. Music instead of dissonance.

Lisa and Donna looked at one another and smiled.

"Taylor," Donna said needlessly as a bit of pride pricked at her.

Lisa nodded. "I'd say that Frank was a bit of a miracle worker. In my book, that gets him invited to dinner."

Donna knew that her sister-in-law was right. For this effort, she could at least feed him. "It's not dinner I'm worried about."

Lisa knew. She patted Donna's cheek. "One step at a time, Donna. One step at a time."

"*That's* what I'm worried about," Donna replied. That first step was a killer.

Chapter Five

He was blending in well. Almost too well.

At dinner Frank had kept everyone entertained. Dinner, never a quiet affair with Stephen and Taylor at the table, had turned into a contest of one-upmanship between the two boys. Each had tried to snare Frank's exclusive attention as well as his approval. Taylor's semisurly attitude had all but vanished, disappearing as if it had never existed. Stephen was behaving like a puppy, eager to be petted.

Frank had managed to satisfy both of them. Donna couldn't help but admire that.

Lisa couldn't have been more pleased. "I think he's the best thing since thirty-one flavors of ice cream were invented," she confided to Donna in a whisper as she picked up the dishes and carried them into the other room.

"You would," Donna muttered.

She followed Lisa into the kitchen with a fistful of silverware that she'd had to practically wrestle away from Frank when he offered to help. She set the utensils down on the stoppered sink with a clatter and then took out the bottle of lemon-scented dish-washing detergent from beneath the counter.

When Donna turned on the water, Lisa looked at her in exaggerated utter horror. "What are you doing?"

Donna thought that it was rather obvious. She squirted the detergent under the stream of water. Foam began rising. "The dishes."

Lisa clamped her hand over the tap, closing it. "We have a dishwasher for things like that." She raised a sarcastic brow. "Or haven't you noticed?"

With a smile, Donna pried Lisa's hand from the faucet and turned the water back on. "Nothing beats cleaning by hand."

As a lawyer, there were times that Lisa had to stubbornly dig in and stick to her guns. It came in handy at moments like this. "If you were any younger, I'd apply my hand and it would be to a specific place on your anatomy, not a dish." Plunging her own hand into the sink, she retrieved the stopper and yanked it out. The water sighed as it drained out, leaving behind sporadic peaks of virgin suds. "Go, mingle. I'll take care of drudgery."

She didn't want to go. She wanted to remain here, with the dishes and with Lisa, where it was safe. Where longings didn't have an avenue open to them. "I—"

Lisa's eyes narrowed. Like a melodramatic villain foreclosing on the old homestead and sending Little Nell off into the snow, she pointed with her wet hand toward the doorway. *"Go."*

Stonewalled, Donna left.

Frank was sitting with Taylor, playing the guitar. When she saw the two of them together, she had the oddest feeling of déjà vu. As if she'd been there before and witnessed this very same scene at some other time.

But of course she hadn't. She'd never seen Frank before this day. Yet Frank could play the guitar just the way Tony had and it didn't take a wild stretch of her imagination to imagine Tony sitting there with Taylor.

Knowing that to leave would be rude, Donna sat down and listened.

And was completely swept away against her will. Frank could do things with a guitar she hadn't thought possible.

Strumming it, he could almost make it weep. He certainly could make it sing. Song after song poured forth, upon request from the boys and, reluctantly, from her.

"That's the song I want to do," Taylor declared after Frank had played the song Donna had asked for. "Greensleeves."

Frank glanced at Donna's face. He saw a mixture of pain woven through the pleasure. The song meant something to her, he thought. Perhaps more than a little. He raised his brow. "All right with you?"

It had been their song—Tony's and hers. It had been playing on the radio when Tony had kissed her for the first time in his father's old car. They had just been sitting and talking, when he'd suddenly leaned over and kissed her. An oldies rendition of "Greensleeves" had come on just at that moment.

Let it go a small voice within her whispered.

Oh, great, now she was hearing Lisa in her head, Donna thought. But the sentiment still made sense. She did have to let go of some things, especially if it was important to Taylor. "All right with me."

Frank nodded and began the task of showing Taylor where to place his fingers on the frets.

After an evening of intensified drilling, Taylor could find pieces of the tune on the guitar. His strumming had become less heavy-handed and his enthusiasm was tempered and manageable. Taylor had made a lot of progress in a relatively short amount of time.

Even he was surprised.

Just as Frank finished placing a call for a cab, Lisa began herding her nephews out of the room. "Okay, boys, off to bed."

Stephen wiggled in protest as she took his hand. "But it's not a school night, Aunt Lisa."

"Never mind," Lisa chided. "Your mommy wants to talk to Mr. Harrigan." She glanced at Donna significantly. "Alone."

Donna cringed inwardly. There was absolutely nothing subtle about Lisa.

A little of Taylor's earlier suspicions returned. He looked from Frank to his mother, not certain if he liked the idea of the two of them together.

"About what?"

"If she wanted you to know," Lisa said, nudging Taylor toward the doorway, "she would say it in front of you, now wouldn't she?"

It made sense, but it didn't satisfy his curiosity. "But—"

Lisa leapt right in. Two years of on-the-job training had made her an expert at outmaneuvering her nephews. "Yes, get that part of your body into bed—posthaste."

Stephen looked up and giggled as he left the room. "You talk funny."

"No flattery, hotshot." She gave him a friendly swat on his seat. "Just get into your pajamas." Lisa turned and looked over her shoulder at Frank. "This is going to take a while, so I'll say good-night now."

Donna closed her eyes, mortified. Lisa had all but waved a red flag and shot off a starter pistol. The edginess returned as soon as the others walked out into the hall.

"Good night," Frank called after Lisa and the departing boys. Taylor echoed the words and Stephen waved.

Frank set the guitar carefully aside next to his suitcase and then turned toward Donna. "Lisa said you wanted to talk to me?" When Donna made no response, he prodded further. "About what?"

Donna shrugged helplessly. "You'll have to ask Lisa. She's the one who came up with the scenario."

This was ridiculous. She was a grown, capable woman, a single mother, the owner of a charter service. She paid people's salaries, for heaven's sake. Why did she have this insane desire to get up and flee?

He was on the sofa and she was on the love seat. One of them was going to have to move, and it was obvious that it wasn't going to be her. Frank rose.

Donna could feel the pulse in her throat and wrists jumping as Frank crossed the small space. His thigh brushed against hers as he sat down next to her. Donna searched for something to say. "Lisa seems to think I should go out more."

"More," he repeated, his eyes slowly gliding along her face. She felt as if he had touched her. "As in going out more often or going out in the first place?"

Donna stared straight ahead, plotting ways to get even with Lisa for putting her in this predicament. "In the first place."

"I see." Frank nodded, wondering how long she could continue talking to the television set. Experimentally, he toyed with the tendrils at her temple. "Well, she and I are in complete agreement. You should go out." Donna turned to look at him. "With me."

She felt her mouth going dry. He was so close to her, she could feel his breath on her face. She tried to remember promises she had made to herself. "I don't want you to get the wrong idea, Frank—"

Lightly he combed his fingers through her hair and brushed it away from her cheek. "I don't have any ideas at all yet, but I'm working on them."

Excitement, sudden and charged, filled him the way it never had before. This was something special, he thought. *She* was something special.

Donna had to struggle to keep her eyes from fluttering shut. With flagging determination, she shifted as far away as she could on the love seat. It amounted to an inch at best. Not nearly enough room to protect her from her own stirred emotions.

Her eyes strayed to the guitar. "I appreciate what you're doing for Taylor," she said a little too quickly.

"He's a good kid. Good kids deserve a break." Frank looked at Donna. He wanted to hold her, to kiss her, to feel her body heat against his. "No matter what their age."

Donna laced her hands together, as if joining them could somehow give her the strength she needed. "You told me a lot about yourself at the airport," she began hesitantly, searching for words.

He had done a little too much talking then, but it was only to coax her out of her shell. "One of us had to talk."

She conceded the point. "All right, let me tell you something about me now. Tony was my high school sweetheart." She stopped as a self-deprecating smile curved her mouth. A mouth he longed to kiss. "Corny, isn't it?"

It didn't sound corny to him; it sounded sweet. Like her. "Hey, you can't tell by me. I'm from Oz, remember? Where I come from, people still occasionally trade poultry for medical help."

Donna smiled. He was making this easier whether he meant to or not. "Anyway, when I married him, I thought it was going to last forever." Memories darkened her eyes. "Forever was exactly seven years." *And then he ended it. He took a wonderful, vibrant life and ended it.*

Donna looked at Frank, trying to make him understand. It was important to her that he did. That she push him away as gently as possible.

"My parents died in a car accident when I was twenty-two. And then when Tony died, I started to feel as if I couldn't hold on to anyone I loved. It made committing difficult, so...I...didn't." She stretched out the words, then shrugged as she hurried to continue. "It seemed easier that way. Taylor and Stephen are the only men in my life now. There's no room for anything else. For anyone else." She bit her lip. This wasn't easy for her. She didn't like to expose her inner feelings, and she had stopped short of mentioning the suicide because the word still wouldn't work its way out of her mouth. Besides, there was no need for Frank to know about that. "Am I making this clear?"

"Painfully." But he remained seated where he was, inches away from her. He noticed that she hadn't mentioned how her husband had died. Now wasn't the time to ask. "Since your mind is made up, you wouldn't mind if I hung around a little and gave it my best shot, would you?"

She didn't understand. "Your best shot?" she repeated.

He grinned at her. "Are you asking for a demonstration?"

"I—" Her voice didn't seem to be doing what she wanted it to.

"—because I'd love to work up to it." Frank placed his fingertips along her cheek, caressing it softly.

Donna felt heat rushing to where he was touching her, detailing the spot with a faint red outline. Her breath caught in her throat, holding back her protests like a dam in a river.

Desire and fear mingled in her eyes, the look at once pleading for him to stop as it begged for him to continue.

Frank followed his own instincts. He brought his mouth down to hers so lightly, she thought she only imagined the contact.

Imagined it and wished it.

His mouth moved over hers, the movement as soft as a rose petal floating to the silken water's edge. Slowly, by tiny degrees, the kiss deepened, dragging her beneath the water's surface into a wondrous world of swirling emotions and blinding lights. She couldn't breathe, she couldn't think.

All she could do was feel.

Cupping his hand beneath her head, Frank drew her closer, surrendering to the urge of losing himself in the tastes and sensations that had opened up to him without warning. They held him in their collective palm, leaving him in awe. He tasted her needs, her bottled-up emotions, and was humbled by it. Humbled and more excited than he'd thought was humanly possible from a mere touching of the lips.

Donna wove her hands into his hair as if to prove to herself that this incredible feeling was real. Sensation after sensation battered her like waves pounding against the beach as the intensity of the kiss heightened.

She'd had no idea how much she had been holding back until it all broke free. She'd had no idea how hungry she was until she had sampled a morsel at the banquet table.

Tears twined themselves with a surge of joy inside her. She felt her very bones melting, felt everything melting, running together like a rainbow in a slick of oil on the ground.

Just as his easygoing manner had done at the airport earlier, his mouth was now coaxing things from her, coaxing responses from her she had no intentions of giving until she gave them.

Now he knew.

Now Frank knew why something had all but whispered in his ear, urging him to heed Greg's invitation, to come to this city, to this place. It was so that he could meet Donna. So that he could be right here, right now, in the center of this wondrous whirlwind he found himself in, this amusement park ride he had no control over.

Fate had somehow arranged it. And he was everlastingly grateful to fate.

She was feeling again. Feeling when she had sworn to herself that she wouldn't.

She couldn't. Mustn't. All of that belonged in the past, in another lifetime—the life that wasn't hers anymore.

Fear chewed a hole in the tapestry that surrounded her and let the cold air rush in.

Donna pulled back, afraid of what she was experiencing. Afraid of herself. Afraid of this man who was making it all begin again.

Frank saw the fear entering Donna's eyes and didn't push. But neither could he force himself to release her, not just yet.

She could hear her heart beating in her ears, rushing, yearning. "Frank, I—"

"Shh. Just a little longer. Let me hold you a little longer." His breathing was steadying, but not nearly as quickly as he would have liked. He really hadn't been prepared for this. "Just until I get the use of my legs back." He looked down into her eyes. "You pack a hell of a punch, you know that?"

Still trembling, Donna pressed her lips together, inadvertently sealing in the imprint of his mouth. "I didn't mean to—"

Did she have any idea how incredibly sweet she was? He was tempted to kiss her all over again, but knew that, for now, he couldn't. For some reason, she was afraid. Kissing her again so soon would be like cleaning a rifle in front of a deer.

"Whether you meant to or not, you did." He wanted her and it was scrambling his brains something fierce. "Since there's no room in your life for anyone else, do you mind if I set up camp outside and hope?"

"What?"

He shook his head and waved his words away. "Never mind."

He didn't know if he was making any sense. He knew he didn't feel very sensible. He felt as if he were a tiny sailing vessel that had just been tossed around in an incredibly fierce typhoon and had barely escaped with his life.

Frank took a deep breath, then smiled at her. The cab would be coming for him soon. He rose, then crossed to the sofa and picked up his suitcase. "You were going to give me the name of a good hotel in the area."

She nodded, grateful for the opportunity to try a simple task. She wasn't up to anything more complex right now, for instance, anything that required thinking. Frank had succeeded in completely stripping her mind down to nothing.

She paused, trying to remember the name of the hotel she passed each day on the way home. "The Alhambra on Fifth and Sandtree," she told him as she led the way to the front door.

He followed her. It seemed as if he were following a faint trail of perfume. "Is it close?"

Donna stopped and turned to face him. She knew it was a mistake the instant she did it. "Yes."

He gave in to temptation and touched her face once more, then dropped his hand. Another second and he'd take her back into his arms. "Then maybe I can see you again while I'm in Seattle?"

Donna looked up into his eyes and instantly felt herself getting lost. She concentrated on forming each word of her reply. "Taylor will be counting on it. I think he needs more than one lesson."

His grin was broad and utterly unsettling. "Then that makes two of us."

She knew what he was saying, and it was time she made herself clear. "Frank, I don't want to go back on the merry-

go-round." She didn't want to fall in love. Love came with
a price and she couldn't bear to pay it again. "I can't."

He heard a car horn beeping and knew it was for him.
Still, he lingered just a second longer. "Why not? This time
you may get the brass ring." If what he felt at this moment
was real, he could practically guarantee it.

She opened the door. "That's your cab, Frank. You'd
better go. Good night."

"Good night," he echoed. Just before she closed the
door, he pressed a kiss to his fingertip and then slid it along
her lip. He watched desire spring into her eyes again, despite her safeguards. He smiled. "I'll see you in the morning."

"All right."

Donna shut the door. She should have said no. She should
have said she was going to be busy. In fact, if she had any
sense at all, she would be gone when he came tomorrow
morning.

Donna sighed as she leaned against the door and ran her
fingers along her lips. They were still throbbing.

If she had any sense at all...

The Hotel Alhambra, with its dark mahogany trim and its
heavy wooden furniture, reminded Frank of the time he had
spent in Baja, California. He liked the Mexican atmosphere. The Alhambra was clean, reasonable and, most important of all, close to Donna. He gave the desk clerk the
necessary information, produced his charge card and was
rewarded with a key within five minutes.

His room was on the seventh floor. Seven had always been
a lucky number for him.

He rode up the elevator with a newlywed couple who
could barely wait to reach the honeymoon suite to begin
their marriage. It only made him think of Donna. And
yearn.

Letting himself into his room, he placed his suitcase on
the small desk and then flopped down on the bed. Exhaustion had finally caught up to him. He stared at the ceiling
and could have sworn that he saw the outline of Donna's

face in the shadows that were being cast across it by the lights coming from a neighboring building.

All in all, it had been an interesting day, he mused. A *hell* of an interesting day.

Belatedly, he remembered that he had promised to call Jeannie when he arrived in Seattle.

He sat up wearily and reached for the telephone. Dragging it over, he rested it on his lap and tapped the numbers on the keypad that would connect him to his sister's home. He counted six rings before the receiver was finally picked up.

A very sleepy voice murmured, "Hello?"

He settled back against the headboard, making himself comfortable. "Boy, some doctor you are. If I was an emergency case, I would have died by now."

"That's okay." Jeannie sounded completely wide-awake now. It was a talent she had cultivated over the years. "I would have brought you back. No extra charge." He heard a male voice in the background. Shane, undoubtedly asking who it was. "I don't know," she answered the voice. "Shane wants to know where you are, Frank. We'd just about given up on you."

"At the Alhambra Hotel."

That didn't sound right. "Why aren't you at Greg's apartment? Did he throw you out already?" She didn't tell Frank that she had had more than a few anxious moments, wondering what had happened to him and why he hadn't called. She'd called the number he had left with her and gotten no answer. Frank might be her older brother, but that didn't stop her from worrying about him whenever he was away.

He filled her in regarding Greg's odd disappearance and the sudden business trip.

She sounded confused. "So why aren't you on your way home?"

Where did he begin the story? It felt as if so much had happened in such a short amount of time. "I met this woman on the flight over—"

Well, that would explain everything. "Boy, you don't waste any time, do you?"

He knew what it sounded like but for once, he was innocent. At least in the beginning. "It wasn't exactly my doing. She fell into my lap."

Jeannie thought back to their years in school and then to the present. Even now, more than one patient came to the clinic with a complaint merely to have Frank take her blood pressure and pulse. "They usually do."

"No, I mean literally." He tried again. "There was turbulence."

She laughed. "I bet there was."

He blew out a breath, exasperated. "Are you going to be serious?"

"That depends." There had been something in Frank's voice, something different. Jeannie was sure of it. "Are you?"

"I don't know," he told her honestly. All this was happening so fast. He was accustomed to being attracted to a woman, not magnetized. It was almost as if he didn't have any say in the matter. "Since I'm here, I think I'll stick around for a while, in case Greg returns as suddenly as he was called away."

"Uh-huh." It wasn't Greg he was interested in, she thought, but that was all right. Jeannie had somehow known when he had told her about this trip that it wasn't going to be a simple matter. "Good thing I got in contact with a nursing agency today. They're sending someone over tomorrow morning."

Frank laughed. Jeannie never let things get away from her. "Boy, talk about not wasting any time—"

"I had a premonition about this."

"Oh? What kind of a premonition?" Maybe she could shed some light on this, because he sure couldn't. He felt as if he were smack in the middle of a dream.

"Just a feeling, that's all." Frank could almost hear her shrugging. "I thought there had to be some kind of a reason for you going, something more compelling than a letter from an old friend. And, if there was, that you might be staying longer than either one of us thought. Sometimes things just seem to happen, to fall into place, that we have no control over."

She thought of her own life, of the events that had seemed to dovetail just so, so that she and Shane could be brought together. If any of the pieces had been missing, she'd be lying alone in her bed tonight. And there wouldn't be a precious little boy sleeping in the next room.

Frank thought of the almost irresistible urge he'd had to come here, of the lost reservation and the pregnant woman who had needed his help. Both his and Donna's help. "Yeah, tell me about it."

"So, is she pretty?"

"She's past pretty and on her way to gorgeous." He laughed again and the sound gladdened Jeannie's heart. This one, she thought, was going to be different. This one was going to count. She had a feeling . . .

"I see. Well, if anything serious *does* develop, I want to check her out for myself. I don't give away my big brother to just anyone, you know."

She'd tried to run his life ever since she was old enough to talk. At times it irritated him. Most of the time it made him feel loved. Nevertheless . . . "Tell Shane he's not doing his job and keeping you in line. You're getting too big for your britches again."

"My britches fit just fine, thank you. And you always needed me to look after you, and you know it." Shane was inching his hand along her thigh and Jeannie was beginning to lose the thread of her thoughts. "Well, enjoy yourself while I'm slaving away here."

That much, he knew, was true. His sister worked much too hard. "I fully intend to. Kiss Mollie and Johnny for me."

"I will." She covered her husband's hand with her own to stop him from questing. Just until she hung up. "Oh, Mollie says she wants you to bring her back a souvenir book on the history of Seattle."

That was typical. "Sometimes I think that girl's too intelligent for her own good."

She grinned, pleased. Mollie had taught herself to read at the age of four because she'd been too impatient to wait until someone could read to her. "She comes by it naturally."

"I see that marriage certainly hasn't done anything for your modesty."

Jeannie laughed as she sank happily back into bed and against Shane. "No, but it's made me very happy. You should try it sometime."

Lately that was beginning to sound like a less frightening concept than it used to. "I'll keep that in mind. Good night, Jeannie."

"Good night. Oh, and Frank?"

He had almost hung up. "Yes?"

Jeannie's voice softened. "Stay in touch."

He thought it was an odd thing for her to say since he would be returning to Wilmington Falls in two weeks or so, but he agreed, anyway. Jeannie pretended not to be, but she was a worrier.

When he hung up and lay down again, the shadows on the ceiling were still there.

And they still looked like Donna.

Chapter Six

Donna couldn't fall asleep. The past eighteen hours or so had reversed polarities in her world. All her emotions had been tossed, headlong, into a blender and scrambled. It left her so keyed up, she began to doubt that she would ever fall asleep again.

There, in the darkness of her own room, as she tossed and turned in her double bed, she relived that kiss over and over again until it seemed a feature length movie instead of one tiny instant in time.

Guilt became her bedfellow.

Since Tony had died, she hadn't even remotely entertained the possibility of being with another man. She hadn't so much as *looked* at one. Now she was not only looking, she was longing. And leaving herself open to a great deal of disappointment in the bargain.

In all likelihood, Frank Harrigan wouldn't be back.

And in her heart, she knew that would be the best thing for her.

All night long, her thoughts bounced back and forth over the tennis net, first being lobbed to one side, then the other. Neither satisfied her.

By two o'clock, exhausted by her emotional waffling, Donna's eyes finally slid closed and she fell into a fitful, restless sleep. The rest of the night was smeared with fragments of dreams that faded almost before they formed.

The chimes of a doorbell infiltrated the seams of her sleep, throbbing impatiently until her mind finally rose to the surface and she woke up. Donna pried her eyes open, feeling a good deal more dead than alive. The sound of the doorbell didn't fade away. It continued ringing. Insistently.

It was *her* doorbell.

Straggling out of bed, Donna shook off the sheet that had somehow gotten tightly wrapped around her leg during her night of tossing and stumbled out of her bedroom. Thoughts of justifiable homicide were sprouting like unchecked weeds in her head.

She was the last one up. The children, who normally had to be practically dynamited out of bed Monday through Friday to get ready for school, were up of their own accord and, by the sounds of it, raring to go. The television set was on. Yosemite Sam was threatening some varmint in the living room for no one's entertainment. Stephen and Taylor weren't there. Donna heard the boys talking, their voices shuffling and reshuffling into one another's. Lisa's voice was raised above theirs.

She thought they were arguing, then realized that they were talking to someone, and it wasn't the housekeeper.

Angelina was in the kitchen. The woman lifted a brow as she critically appraised the football jersey Donna had slept in. "I would put on more than that if I were you."

Donna groaned as she dragged a hand through her hair. "We have company?"

One side of Angelina's thin mouth raised in a half smile. "Oh, yes, and he can certainly keep me company anytime."

"He?" Donna was afraid to form a thought, but it came anyway. No, it couldn't be. Not again. Not so soon.

The other corner of the woman's mouth rose, as well. Angelina, mother of two, grandmother of five, was transformed into a lively twenty-year-old as she nodded. "Very much a 'he.'"

Donna sighed and followed the voices to the family room. Déjà vu.

Donna blinked, then stared at Frank. He was standing in the middle of the room, surrounded by the rest of her family. It was a replay of last night except that there was no suitcase in sight. And she was wearing what passed for her nightgown. Donna pushed back a wave of exasperated embarrassment. "Didn't you go home last night? Or at least to a hotel?"

She looked cute, rumpled. One side of the football jersey was rising temptingly on her thigh. A man could learn a lot about a woman by the way she looked first thing in the morning. Frank had no complaints. Her eyes were still smoky with sleep, her hair slightly mussed and all in all, she looked irresistible.

"I did," he told her. "And it's a very nice hotel at that."

"Only the finest for Seattle," she mumbled.

The way he was looking at her made her long for a robe, or better yet, something that couldn't be pierced by X-ray vision. He made her feel as if she weren't wearing anything. Donna lifted her chin, determined to brazen it out. "If you like the hotel so well, what are you doing here?"

The look in his eyes answered her question. Donna tugged the jersey down self-consciously.

An innocent smile lifted the corners of his mouth. "I thought I'd take you all out to breakfast in exchange for services rendered."

"Services?" she asked slowly, trying to make sense out of the word as Taylor and Stephen cried, "All right!" and high-fived each other.

There was still a fog wrapped around her brain. She wasn't good on her feet first thing in the morning. It usually took two cups of coffee to activate her brain and bring her around to joining the world of the living.

He could see the confusion and suspicion etched across her brow. "Services," he repeated. "As in taking me sightseeing." Frank hooked his thumbs on the front of his jeans.

"I know that the Space Needle's supposed to be around here somewhere, but I don't have a clue as to where."

No one could get that lost. "Downtown," she replied. "You can't miss it."

Angelina entered the room, drawn by the conversation. Or possibly her appreciation for a good-looking man. Donna tried to ignore her.

The look Frank gave Donna made her curl her bare toes into the carpet. "I don't like to do things alone," he told her.

"Well, then," Lisa began, riding to the rescue before Donna could turn him down, "you've come to the right place." She threaded her arms through Frank's to divert his attention from the scowl she saw forming on Donna's face. "Donna was just telling me last night that she can never get enough of the sights that Seattle has to offer."

Donna's mouth dropped open as she stared in disbelief at her sister-in-law.

"Actually," Frank told Lisa, playing along as he looked at the boys, who were hanging on very word, "I was thinking of taking everyone."

Stephen was already jumping up and down, anticipating a positive answer. "Us, too?" Eagerness highlighted his heart-shaped face.

"You, too," Frank said, nodding. Then he turned to the woman at his side. "And Lisa."

The last thing she wanted to do was get in the way. Or be used as a buffer by Donna. She knew her sister-in-law too well. Lisa dropped her hands from his arm and shook her head. "No, I—"

"Yes, Lisa," Donna said suddenly.

There was safety in numbers. If she were to be sucked into this, like a mote of dust into a vacuum cleaner, she wanted Lisa to be there. She knew that it might seem ridiculous, but she felt unaccountably nervous. Donna didn't want to be alone with Frank, was *afraid* to be alone with Frank. The more people there were between them, the better.

Lisa began to beg off in earnest, then relented. If she came along, she could entertain the boys and provide Donna with an opportunity to be with Frank. It might work out after all.

"Mister," Lisa said, "you just bought yourself some tour guides."

"Great." He turned toward Donna. "Would you like to change, or do you feel comfortable coming along the way you are?"

Wise guy. "I'll change." She turned on her bare heel and marched back into her room.

"Good decision." Frank's voice trailed after her.

"I *really* don't think so," Donna muttered under her breath, but she was outnumbered.

And perhaps not fighting it as hard as she ought to.

Stephen and Taylor both wanted to go to a local fast-food restaurant that served hot cakes and sausages in the blink of an eye. It made no difference to Frank, but he had a suspicion that Lisa and Donna would have preferred something that wasn't getting a tan beneath a hundred-watt bulb. It was Donna's groan that gave him the clue.

Tactfully, he suggested that they compromise between their choice and a regular, more atmosphere-oriented restaurant. They wound up having breakfast at an internationally famous restaurant for internationally famous pancakes. A ton of them, it turned out.

Frank watched, amused, as Stephen polished off a short stack. It was his second and the boy gave no signs of being full.

Frank leaned over toward Donna and asked in an audible, exaggerated whisper, "Are you sure he doesn't have a tapeworm?"

Stephen paused, his lower lip jutting out. "I don't have any worms. I keep asking Mom for a pet snake, but she won't let me have one because she says I'd have to feed it live worms."

Donna shivered at the very thought of it. With Stephen's penchant for losing things, the snake would be slithering around the house in no time.

"Stephen's always been a good eater. And he seems to burn it off before he gets up from the table." Tony had been like that, she remembered. Blessed with a metabolism that never stopped going. "It runs in the family."

"I noticed." Frank smiled when she looked at him quizzically. "Yours seem to have burned off quite nicely."

It was just a compliment. Nothing she hadn't heard before. If anything, his was less blatantly stated. No reason to be affected. But there was something genuine about his words, his manner. She'd had men flirt with her before. They'd flirted with Donna McCullough, savvy businesswoman. But no one had ever flirted with Taylor and Stephen's mom. Until now.

Maybe that was why she could feel the color rising to her cheeks.

"So," she began a little too briskly as she folded her hands in front of her empty coffee cup, "is there anywhere in particular that you'd like to go?"

A dark, intimate movie theater where we could neck in the last row. The thought brought a smile to his mouth. He hadn't done anything like that since he was seventeen. But there was something about Donna that made him want to go back to his youth and relive it again. With her.

Donna felt herself growing warmer, knowing that whatever Frank said wasn't what he was actually thinking. She could see that in his eyes.

He smiled as he watched her blush bloom. "Why don't we begin with Fun Forest Amusement Park?"

Donna pressed her lips together as her sons cheered the choice. This bewildered, lost tourist act of Frank's was just that. An act. If nothing else, the man had a guidebook at his disposal.

She tried to be irritated, but couldn't. Still, she pinned him with a look. "You couldn't have just pulled that out of a hat."

He shrugged his shoulders guilelessly. "Lucky guess?" he suggested.

Her eyes narrowed. "I thought you wanted to see the Space Needle."

He had given that some thought over breakfast. "Let's leave that for last. I hear they've got a great restaurant there and that the view is spectacular at night."

Donna felt as if she were heading downhill on a toboggan that was out of control. "Whoa." She held up her hand. "You're talking about spending the entire day together."

If she meant to accuse him of overstepping his boundaries, he gave no indication that he understood. He sipped the last of his coffee and looked at Donna's face. "Yes. Any objections?"

"Nope," Taylor said before his mother had a chance to respond.

"None," Lisa said with equal feeling. She purposely avoided looking at Donna.

Stephen was already on his feet, ready to run off. "Let's go."

Donna dug in, though she knew it was useless. She had to protest for form's sake if nothing else. This man couldn't just waltz into their lives from nowhere and monopolize their whole day. "Hey, wait a minute. Don't I get a say in this?"

"Sure," he agreed. "As long as whatever you say has the word *yes* in it."

The discussion that rose in her mind belonged in private, but she didn't have the luxury. She settled on giving him a summarized form. "Frank, you're moving too fast."

His grin was sensual and permeated her skin like heat rising from a hot bath. The fact that her family was all around her didn't seem to weaken its effect or insulate her from it. It only saved her from surrendering to it completely.

"Lady," he promised Donna as she signaled for the check, "you ain't seen nothin' yet."

She knew he was right.

Donna felt like someone on the top step of a platform after the plane had taxied away. She was tottering and liable to fall off at any second.

Donna yielded. Just as everyone knew she would. "All right. We'll go to the park and see the Space Needle later."

He grinned as he placed his charge card on the plate next to the bill the waitress brought. The waitress hurried away with it. "Good choice."

"Do you always get your way?" Donna wanted to know, smarting.

"Enough times to make me hopeful," he answered evasively.

He was a damn sight more than hopeful, she thought grudgingly.

But hopeful of what, she wasn't certain.

That settled, Frank launched into a dialogue with her sons of the merits of Bugs Bunny's antics as compared to Garfield's. His stock with the boys went up another ten notches.

Donna merely shook her head. The man was not real.

Taylor and Stephen dragged Frank from one of the park's nineteen rides to another. Donna had tried to hang back, but no one would let her. There was a conspiracy going on against her. Lisa, Taylor, Stephen and Frank—most especially Frank—were on one side and she on the other. There was always someone to grab her hand and pull her along, to wedge her beside Frank when they went down Windstorm. She clutched at his arm as they sailed down a fifty-foot drop, a scream ripping from her without permission.

She was embarrassed, and he only laughed, amused. Which made her angry. But she didn't have time to remain that way because there was another ride to go on, another sight to see.

A good deal of the time, Frank took her hand and drew her to him.

As they all crossed and recrossed the six-acre park, it evolved into an afternoon of laughter and casual touching with not-so-casual results.

She was enjoying him, she thought. Enjoying him, and she didn't want to. Didn't want any of this mad rushing feeling to be happening again.

She was afraid.

When the day finally wound down and Donna and Lisa dropped down on the grass to rest, Frank roughhoused with Taylor and Stephen less than a few yards away.

Lisa laughed, watching. "I've never seen so much energy in one place before."

Stephen shrieked and, laughing, Frank pulled him down and tickled him. Taylor leapt up to pin Frank the way he'd seen wrestlers do on television. Frank pretended to be over-powered.

God, it was wonderful to see them so happy. "I guess the boys have been storing it up."

"I was talking about Frank." Lisa looked at Donna. "He's pretty amazing."

Donna nodded. His energy seemed limitless. She certainly couldn't have kept up with her sons and still been able to wrestle with them the way he was doing now.

"Yes, that's the word for it all right." She smiled, drawing her knees to her chest and resting her chin on them. "I guess they miss having a man around." The old familiar ache tiptoed through her. "Tony used to do that with them." She nodded toward the field. "Take them to the park on Sundays and chase them until they all dropped, exhausted."

"I remember." Lisa's expression grew serious. "You know, Donna—"

Donna tensed. She recognized that tone. The words that were going to follow undoubtedly weren't words that she wanted to hear. "Drop it."

Lisa grew slightly defensive. "I haven't said anything yet."

Donna merely raised a brow and looked at her. "Your tone did."

Lisa debated letting it go and decided that she wouldn't be a friend if she did. That would have been the easy route. Lisa wasn't much for easy.

"Well, now that you've got the melody, let me at least give you the words." She saw a warning look enter Donna's eyes, but doggedly continued. "You really should start thinking about remarrying and giving the boys a father."

Donna's expression sobered. How could Lisa say something like that? She was Tony's sister. "They *have* a father."

Lisa wasn't about to back down. "All right," she conceded gamely, "a cuddly playmate, then." She moved closer, lowering her voice. She didn't want Frank to overhear. "They need a man in their lives and so do you."

Donna blew out a breath and turned her attention toward the activity a few feet away. Frank had Stephen on his shoulders, with Taylor yelling, cheering them on. It was hard to shut that out.

She tried anyway. "No, they need love in their lives and I'd like to think that you and I supply that in abundance."

Lisa was silent for a moment and Donna thought the argument was over. But then she asked, "All right, how about you?"

Donna looked at her. "How about me what?"

She was being intentionally obtuse, Lisa thought, determined to force Donna into admitting that her life wasn't complete. That she needed to be loved and to love. "Don't you need love in your life?"

Donna looked at her sons. They were more than enough for her. "I'm getting it."

"I mean from someone old enough to vote, Donna. You're still a very young woman—"

"I said to drop it, Lisa." Donna fairly ground out the warning.

Lisa prided herself on knowing when to pick up the pieces in order to fight another day. She raised her hands in surrender. "I just hate seeing someone I care about missing out."

Humor returned to her eyes as Donna looked at Lisa. "And I hate to see someone *I* care about nursing a black eye, so don't tempt me to give you one, okay?"

Lisa ran the tip of her tongue along her lip, amused. "My, my, violent when we're sensitive, aren't we?"

"Don't push," Donna advised.

The next moment, she was being attacked on two fronts as Taylor and Stephen came charging at her and then collapsed beside her in heaps, laughing, too breathless to form any coherent words.

Frank dropped down next to Donna as Stephen scooted over to give him room. "Whatever you've been feeding these kids, I think the government should know about it. We'd wind up with a hell of a fighting force."

He was too close. With space between them, he was still too close. The breeze shifted and she could detect his dark, manly scent. It was uncomfortably arousing.

Donna looked at her disheveled children, their arms outstretched, lying on the grass, looking as if they couldn't be induced to move for any reason.

"Maybe we should just call it a day," she suggested hopefully.

Frank looked up at the sun. It had begun to set, gold pooling into violets and blues. The colors shimmered in the sky like the strands of a gossamer veil. He nodded thoughtfully. "All right."

The dead suddenly rose as Stephen scrambled up in protest. "Aw—do we have to?" He looked pleadingly at Frank. Not her, Donna noticed, but Frank. This really was getting out of hand.

Frank continued as if there had been no interruption. "—and start calling it an evening." He looked at Taylor and then Stephen. "Hungry?"

Taylor sat up and nodded.

"You bet!" Stephen cried.

Frank laughed and hugged the little boy to him. It came naturally, as if this was the way things were meant to be. "Why doesn't that surprise me?"

Delighted at the turn of events, Lisa rose to her feet. "Let me go get them cleaned up at the rest stop and then we can go wherever it is that Frank wants to go." She said it as if it were a direct order, then looked over her shoulder at Donna.

With that, she took each nephew by the hand and led them off.

Donna hugged her knees to her as she watched them disappear. "The problem with being part of a family," she said half to Frank and half to herself, "is that I'm constantly being outnumbered." She jerked her head around when he touched her hair.

"You had a leaf." He held it up as evidence.

She was jumpy, he thought and didn't know if that was a good thing or not. He only knew that he felt jumpy himself. Jumpy and edgy and happy. He couldn't completely explain it, but it felt as if that last little piece, that piece he'd felt he'd been missing all his life, was finally being maneuvered into place.

He tossed the leaf aside, his eyes never leaving her face. Her eyes had grown large when he touched her, exciting him. But there wasn't anything he could do about it. Not here. "Maybe you should stop marching to a different tune once in a while and join in."

She raised her chin. "I join in just fine." Donna flushed and then sighed as she ran her hand through her hair. "Sorry, I didn't mean to snap."

He shrugged away her apology. "You're only human."

Why did he have to be like this? He was making it so difficult for her to back away from him. "Don't."

Frank drew his brows together, at a loss. "Don't what?"

"Don't be so agreeable." Donna sighed again. That had sounded really stupid.

A Frisbee came flying out of nowhere. Reacting quickly, Frank pulled Donna toward him. It narrowly missed hitting her, but something else hit instead. They exchanged looks, both aware of the spontaneous combustion that had been ignited.

The next moment an overzealous Irish setter came bounding over. Frank released Donna and picked up the Frisbee. He tossed it into the distance. The dog went chasing after it.

Frank felt his mouth growing dry. A first, he thought. A very first. He had never even reacted this way to women he'd gone to bed with, much less just held.

"Would it help if I yelled and stamped my feet a lot?"

He was laughing at her, she thought. Donna closed her eyes and shook her head, wishing that her pulse wasn't scrambling like a hamster in an exercise wheel. "I meant that you're being too perfect."

He couldn't help laughing. "Now you'd be the first one to accuse me of that."

This wasn't coming out right at all. "The boys like you—"

He smiled. This wasn't news. "I like the boys." And he did. Faster than he'd thought possible.

"They like you too much," she continued, determined to make him understand, determined to get this out right. "I don't want them getting attached."

"Why?"

How could he ask that? It was so clear. "Because." When he said nothing, waiting, she added, "Because you'll be leaving soon and then they'll miss you."

The future was no longer a foregone conclusion. It had gotten clouded from the first moment he had seen her. "Why don't we take it a step at a time, and by the time I'm supposed to leave, we'll see?"

There was nothing *to* see. He'd go his way and they theirs. "See what?"

He heard the boys shouting to him in the distance. Frank wound a strand of her hair around his finger. "Whatever there is to see." He couldn't make it any clearer than that for either of them.

She pulled her hair away. But she was unable to do the same with her eyes. "You're being purposely enigmatic."

He grinned. "So's life."

"I—"

But by then, the boys were returning, ready to be entertained, so she swallowed what she'd been about to say. Temporarily.

Like a nimble cat, Frank rose to his feet. He put his hand out to her, waiting. When Donna wrapped her fingers around his, she had the distinct impression that a bond was being made.

And sealed.

She tried not to think about it.

* * *

The view from the restaurant in the Space Needle was not oversold.

"It's like being on top of the world," Frank said to Taylor and Stephen as they all sat at a table. Below them, the city preened like a sophisticated woman, wearing diamond necklaces and bracelets that gleamed seductively in the night. Frank was unabashedly impressed. "There's nothing to match this where I come from."

"Where do you come from?" Stephen asked suddenly. He gathered himself up on his knees to get a better look at the view.

Donna gently tapped his elbows to get them off the table. With a sigh, Stephen sat back down.

"I've lived the last part of my life in a place called Wilmington Falls." He was met with blank stares on either side. "It's in California."

Taylor thought of the afternoon they'd just spent and forgot to be a bored eleven-year-old going on twenty. "Do they have parks where you live?"

Frank laughed. When his family had moved to Wilmington Falls, it had been so rural, that it had hurt. "Most of it looks like a park."

"Neat!" Stephen's response was so enthusiastic, he almost fell off his chair.

Frank caught him before he could tumble over. "I think so." He looked pointedly at Donna. "But they've got a mall and an airport about twenty miles away just so you don't go into culture shock." He turned his attention to Lisa. "I'd say we have the best of both worlds within our reach."

"Trying to sell us on a little land, Mr. Harrigan?" Donna asked, arching a brow.

"Just selling food for thought," he countered.

For a moment, there was silence.

"Well." When they turned to look at her, Lisa raised her glass of diet soda. "To a great day."

Frank inclined his head. "And a better evening."

Donna looked down into her soda glass as the boys chimed in their agreement. The shrimp salad she'd had for dinner couldn't find a suitable place to rest. Her stomach was churning too much.

Chapter Seven

Frank eased his way in, crossing the threshold as Donna held the front door wide open for him. Stephen, his small chin propped up on Frank's shoulder, was fast asleep in his arms. Exhaustion, a long time in coming, had finally claimed him on the car ride home from the restaurant.

Like a frisky puppy, Taylor threaded his way past his aunt, his mother and Frank, and made a beeline for the family room. He had obviously gotten his second wind. With any luck, it wouldn't last long.

Lisa closed the door as Donna turned to Frank. "Here, I'll take him." Donna placed her hands on Stephen, but Frank shook his head.

"I carried him this far. I can certainly go a few more feet. Just show me where his bedroom is."

Donna dropped her hands and turned to lead the way. She was feeling a little tired herself. And edgy. Very, very edgy. But that had nothing to do with the hectic pace of the day she had just spent and everything to do with the man she had spent it with. Even though she was enjoying herself, there was this pervading feeling of foreboding within her.

Something was going to happen.

However, she had no idea what and waiting for it to happen was taking its toll on her nerves.

She walked into the bedroom Taylor and Stephen shared. The room, usually in a state of chaos and buried beneath layers of toys and clothes, was neat and orderly.

Angelina had been here, Donna thought. Shelves were lined with books that were all facing the right way and toys were safely housed in a toy box the size of a Shetland pony. On the far side of the room stood their bunk beds.

"Stephen takes the bottom bunk," she told Frank. "He's afraid of heights."

"You're kidding." Stephen had been the one who continually insisted on riding the roller coaster, lamenting that Windstorm didn't descend faster or climb higher.

"Selectively afraid," Donna amended.

She pulled back the covers and Frank placed the boy down on the bed. She loosened Stephen's shirt, pulling it out of the waistband. It was half out already. Then she removed his shoes. Everything else could stay as it was. He needed his sleep more than he needed his pajamas. Bending over Stephen, she softly pressed a kiss to his forehead.

"He's going to be disappointed that he conked out," she murmured to Frank as she slipped a sheet over the sleeping child.

They both stood for a moment, looking at Stephen. Donna tried not to think about how right that felt, standing beside Frank, gazing at her son.

Frank shook his head, then laughed. "You know, for a little guy, he's deceptively heavy. Must be all those pancakes he had this morning."

Donna raised a brow. "The pancakes," she agreed in a low whisper. "And the cotton candy, and the hot dogs and the grilled hamburgers and—"

Frank held up his hand to stop her. "You've made your point."

Donna turned on the small baseball night light, then switched off the main one. Quietly she eased the door shut. "For a while there, I was afraid Stephen was going to make *his* point by throwing up."

The light in the hallway was purposely dim. It cast soft shades on the wall, blending their silhouettes together. Frank smiled, wondering if that was a foreshadowing of things to come. "You're only a kid once."

Donna sighed. For just a brief moment, a bittersweet sadness passed over her face. "And once isn't nearly long enough." For childhood was the time for illusions, the time to feel secure and safe.

Frank slipped his arm around her shoulders as they walked to the family room. He did it so naturally, Donna didn't realize it at first, didn't react the way she had mentally rehearsed should the moment occur. It was nothing short of the stealthful infiltrating of her soul. He made things too easy, too comfortable for her.

As the warmth penetrated, she looked up at him.

Her eyes were wide, he thought. And beautiful. "Would you like to be a child again, Donna?"

She shook her head. "Not so much a child, I guess as liking the concept of being taken care of. Once in a while, it would be nice not to have to—"

She stopped abruptly as she realized where her words were heading. Her eyes narrowed. She'd slipped again. "How *do* you do that?"

He didn't understand what she was asking him. "Do what?"

He had to know what she was talking about, Donna thought. "Get me to say things I have no intentions of telling you."

He laughed and the low, sensual sound seeped into her soul. "Easy." He looked down into her eyes. "I listen. You wouldn't say it if somewhere in there—" he glided a fingertip along her temple "—you didn't want to share it."

He was right. But she didn't want to admit it, not to him, not to herself. If she did, it would be the beginning of fissures in her walls, walls she had painstakingly constructed in order to be strong. To *stay* strong, for the boys' sake.

Taylor came to her rescue. He stood in the doorway of the family room, the guitar clutched in his hands like a cherished talisman. He looked sheepishly at Frank, completely

innocent of the fact that he had interrupted something between his mother and the man he had gravitated to so
quickly.

"Could you, maybe show me again?" Taylor looked
down at the frets, as if they were somehow responsible for
his inability to coax the melody from the guitar. "I think I
forgot."

"You didn't forget," Frank assured him easily as he took
the guitar from the boy and motioned him to the family
room. "It's buried in your brain somewhere. You just have
to dig it up again." Taylor looked at him quizzically. Frank
was tempted to ruffle the boy's hair, but didn't. Taylor was
trying his best to be older than his years. "You never forget
anything you've learned."

Frank sat down on the sofa. Maybe it would be easier for
Taylor if he had something tangible to look at that could
guide him. "You have any paper? I can write the notes down
for you."

Taylor was already at the desk, rifling through the drawer.
Donna patiently moved him aside and unearthed an eight-
by-ten pad and a pen. She handed them to Taylor, who
quickly hurried over to Frank.

"You can write music?" he asked in awe.

Frank turned the pad sideways and carefully drew several lines across on the page, forming a staff, then began to
fill it in with notes. "A little."

Taylor cocked his head as he studied the notes that were
being formed. "Gee, is there anything that you *can't* do?"
Admiration pulsed in every word.

Donna cleared her throat. When Frank looked up at her,
she rolled her eyes and he laughed.

It was being laid on a little thick, he thought, but he
couldn't help enjoying it. His gaze returned to Donna. "I'm
trying to find that out."

"I don't think that should be too hard to discover,"
Donna tossed over her shoulder as she left the room.

She heard Frank chuckle softly to himself.

Then the strains of "Greensleeves" floated out into the hall, seeking her out. Donna closed her eyes. Ignoring him was getting harder and harder to do.

To be absolutely fair, Donna gave them some time together. Half an hour, she judged, was quite enough. She returned to the family room, but neither Frank nor Taylor seemed to notice she was there. They were both too caught up in the music lesson. Frank had his hand over Taylor's, showing him the exact fingering. Purposely, he had kept the musical arrangement simple.

Donna didn't want the scene to get to her. But it did, anyway.

This was what a father and son looked like. This was what every boy deserved—a man in his life that could show him the way.

This was what, she thought sadly, Taylor and Stephen would never have. Because she was too afraid.

She cleared the lump that had suddenly materialized in her throat. "It's way past your bedtime, Taylor," she finally announced.

Taylor looked up, startled to see her there. "Aw, Mom, tomorrow's Sunday. I can sleep in."

She had to remain firm. Somewhere along the line, she had to take a stand. Discipline was quickly going downhill. "You've already stayed up an hour later than you normally do, even on a weekend." She bent down and took a close look at his face. Taylor pulled his head away, but she saw what she was looking for. "And it looks as if you're struggling to keep those eyes open." They were puffy and just the slightest bit red.

Taylor stubbornly pressed his lips together, stifling a yawn. "No, I'm not." Unable to help himself, he rubbed one eye, but remained sitting exactly where he was, the guitar braced on his knees.

Frank felt he was caught in the middle of this dispute and it wasn't a good place to be, especially since he didn't want to alienate Donna. He placed his hand on the guitar's neck.

Taylor looked at him questioningly. "Listen to your mother, boy."

Like a fort that was surrendered without a shot, Taylor gave up his hold on the guitar. "Okay. Good night." Within a moment, he'd left the room.

Watching, Donna let out a breath between her teeth that sounded suspiciously like a hiss. She looked far from satisfied.

Setting the guitar to one side, Frank rose. He wanted to touch her. Badly. Instead, he shoved his hands into his back pockets. "Something wrong?"

Yes, something was wrong. She wheeled on him. "When I tell him to go to bed, he digs in. When you tell him, he practically runs off." She gestured toward the doorway in exasperation.

He shrugged. "I'm new. The novelty'll wear off." How was it, he wondered, that after a whole day, he could still smell the slight scent of her perfume? Didn't it ever wear out?

Donna crossed her arms before her. "What if it doesn't?"

He wasn't completely certain he knew what she was getting at. "Excuse me?"

Children had their feelings hurt so easily. And it was hard enough on Taylor and Stephen without a father as it was. "What if the novelty *doesn't* wear off before you leave?"

What if I don't leave?

Frank started, taken completely unaware by the thought that shot through his mind with the swiftness of an arrow let loose in the air. Of course he had to leave. He had a life away from here, responsibilities.

But Donna was here.

She held him immobile, as if she were a powerful magnet and he just a screw, aimlessly tossed in her direction.

Or had it been so aimless?

He couldn't shake the feeling that somehow it hadn't.

Frank gave in to the temptation to touch her. Lightly he skimmed her hair with his fingers. Even that affected them both. He saw the smoky look entering her eyes. A look that was mirrored in his soul. How had all this happened so fast?

One minute the ground was solid, the next, there was a tremor and the earth had rocked, tossing him on his duff, making him feel like a young kid.

"Donna, don't clutter up the path with what ifs. It might keep you from something that you want. Something we both might want," he amended.

Desire was blooming in her eyes. Desire that was followed by wariness. She couldn't seem to separate them, he thought. "You shouldn't turn your back on a possible friendship—" He chose the euphemism, thinking that it was safe for her and safe for him. Part of Frank still sought an escape route from this inevitable path he was treading on, because it was all happening so quickly and it scared him. But that part was progressively growing smaller. "—just because you're afraid it won't last forever," he concluded. His eyes held hers. "Because it just might."

She wondered if he could hear her heart beating. She wondered if Seattle could hear her heart beating. "Meaning us?"

He filled his hands with her hair. "It's an axiom. Apply it any way you see fit."

Though she knew she should pull away, she turned her face up to his. She could feel his breath floating along her skin, exciting her, arousing her and mesmerizing her all at the same time.

The next moment, he would have kissed her, had Taylor not popped back into the room. She sprang away from Frank as if his hands had turned into hot irons. Taylor had eyes only for Frank.

"Will you teach me more tomorrow?" he asked as if he was picking up the thread of a conversation that had never ended.

Frank exhaled. His insides felt shaky. What *was* it she did to him? "I'd love to." He looked at Donna. "May I?"

She stood there, with her son looking at her pleadingly and Frank just looking at her, dissolving kneecaps and will with his green eyes. She sighed. How could she possibly say no?

Donna nodded. "Outnumbered again."

"Thanks, Mom!"

"I'll be here at nine," Frank told Taylor. He could have said dawn and the boy would have eagerly agreed.

"Ten," Donna corrected with determination.

"Ten," Frank conceded. He looked at Taylor, a thought suddenly occurring to him. "Hey, aren't the Mariners in town?" He'd heard it on the radio on the way home from the restaurant.

Taylor's hopeful grin couldn't have been any wider if it had been painted on. "Yeah."

"You like baseball?" It was a needless question. Frank slanted a look at Donna to see how she was taking this. Resigned, he noted. He took it to indicate progress. He was wearing her down.

"Man, do I!" Taylor shifted from foot to foot, dying to ask if Frank could take him to the game.

"Maybe after the lesson, we can take in a game. I'll see about getting tickets," he promised. "I suggest you get to bed, Taylor. Tomorrow's shaping up to be a big day."

"You bet!" Pleased, the boy fairly skipped out of the room.

Frank was usurping Donna's position, taking over when he had no right to. "You did it again."

He turned to look at her. Even if he hadn't felt her displeasure, he could see it in her eyes. "What? Made him happy?"

He was twisting her words, making her out to be some kind of an ogre. Her insecurities rose. It wasn't easy being both mother and father to a pair of boys and still run a business.

"No, I—oh, never mind." Frustrated, she waved away the words and would have left the room if he hadn't caught her by the wrist.

When she looked up at him in surprise, he gathered her into his arms. The anger slowly drained out of her. "It seemed like the right thing to do. When something's right, you go with it."

There were too many similarities. Similarities that made her wary, made her want to retreat quickly before she couldn't anymore. "You're just as impulsive as my husband was."

He didn't want to be compared to someone she had grieved over. He wanted their start to be fresh. "Everyone's different, Donna. Look for the differences."

A little less gently than last time, Frank brought his mouth down to hers.

She hadn't meant to let him kiss her. She hadn't meant to kiss him back.

It had been on her mind all day, barely hidden out of sight, waiting for a chance to spring out.

It was as if he had set a match to a fuse attached to a firecracker. She was the firecracker.

Donna felt everything lighting up inside of her, everything exploding. Blinding bright lights flashed everywhere, encompassing her.

She had absolutely no power to contest this. Her body leaned into his, seeking his warmth as her arms rebelliously tightened around his neck.

She was boneless and pliant against him, wanting only to feel like a woman again.

And so desperately needy that it frightened her.

He had to watch himself or he would greedily take what was hesitantly being offered to him and ruin everything. She needed gentle care, patience. She needed to be cherished.

But she was so sweet, so wondrous, and he felt his blood swimming, churning, demanding. He was only human, perhaps more than he would have thought.

His lips moved over hers, savoring, taking and giving back what he hoped she sought.

She was making him crazy.

One more minute and he wasn't going to be responsible for what happened. Employing superhuman effort, Frank pulled back from the brim of the inevitable before he went tumbling over the edge.

Donna looked up at him as he gently ended their kiss, her eyes dazed. He could see the pulse throbbing in her throat. Frank refrained from pressing a kiss to it, knowing he'd be lost if he did.

"Like I said, when something's right, you go with it."

His hands on her shoulders, Frank drew away, afraid that he would take her here, in the home where her children slept, where her sister-in-law lay in her bedroom only a few feet away. Common sense had very little to do with what he was feeling, but he held on to the shred he still had.

"I'll see you in the morning."

Donna wanted to say no, but the only words that would come out were "All right."

The words were still throbbing in her mind after Frank had left. Donna drew a long, steadying breath. What had come over her? She had known the man only two days, and in that time, she'd been more intimate with him emotionally than she had been with anyone before or since Tony. Men she'd known for years had never affected her this way.

She looked accusingly at the door, envisioning him behind it. Up until two days ago, her mind had been very clear and the path she'd chosen for herself had stretched straight before her. Frank represented curves she wasn't prepared for.

Curves, if she wasn't careful, she would wind up slipping on.

"Is he gone?"

Startled, Donna turned and saw Lisa standing in the family room doorway. *Now* she was here. "Where were you when I needed you?"

Being faithful was all well and good, but being faithful to a memory didn't make any sense, Lisa thought. Not at Donna's age. Not when she had young children to raise.

"Exactly where you needed me to be. Offstage." Lisa nodded toward the front door, a pleased smile graced her mouth. "He wouldn't have kissed you if I were standing in here."

Donna looked at her sister-in-law in surprise. "How did you know he kissed me?"

Lisa moved forward and cupped Donna's chin in her hand and turned her head slightly. "You've got that look in your eyes and those lips have definitely been pressed."

Donna could only shake her head. She didn't like what was happening. She didn't like not being in control. She roamed around the family room, straightening things that Angelina had straightened earlier.

"The only look in my eye is confusion. Who is he, Lisa? I mean, really?" She whirled around, looking at Lisa helplessly. "Who *is* he? What's he doing here?" Donna dragged her hand through her hair. "Why has he suddenly dropped out of the sky smack into my life like this?" The questions agitated her, especially since they had no answers.

Lisa took it all in stride. "Why doesn't matter. What mattered is that he did." She shrugged carelessly. "Maybe your guardian angel realized you needed a man in your life and conjured him up for you."

Donna laughed. "There's far too much devil in Frank's eyes for any guardian angel to have conjured him up." Nothing an angel could have come up with could have excited her this way, she thought.

Lisa saw the flush rise to Donna's face. "You'd be the one to know about that." She patted Donna's cheek affectionately. There were only three years separating them, but Lisa felt very motherly toward Donna. "Enjoy it. Don't fight it so hard." She saw a wary look entering Donna's eyes. She knew what Donna had to be feeling. It was frightening, starting over. But if she didn't venture, she'd never enjoy. "At least explore it a little. We'll all be here for you if it doesn't work out."

Donna shook her head. "Don't you understand? I don't *want* it to work out. It worked out with Tony, and what did it get me?"

"Memories," Lisa answered simply. "Two beautiful kids," she added, then placed her hand on Donna's, as if to take some of the fear away and into herself. "Nothing is forever. The best we can do is hope that love finds us for a little while." She nodded toward the front door again. "You got lucky."

She didn't feel very lucky. She felt as if she were walking a tightrope without a net and with no one to catch her when she fell. When, not if. "Why didn't you ever get married, Lisa?"

Lisa smiled wistfully. "Because *I* didn't get found." She looked at Donna pointedly. "But you did. Don't throw it away."

"Ready?"

Donna looked up as Frank entered the den. He'd been in the family room for the past hour, fielding questions from Stephen as he helped Taylor work on his fingering. "Greensleeves" actually had a fairly decent tempo in the making. Donna had taken advantage of the lull to catch up on her bills and balance her checkbook.

"For what?"

Frank leaned over the desk. "The baseball game, remember?"

She'd been hoping that he had forgotten about that. Maybe he only had tickets for the boys. "You got the tickets?"

"I got the tickets." To confirm, he drew them from his shirt pocket and spread them out on her desk.

Donna raised her eyes to his. "Five?" The man was taking thoughtfulness to a new plateau.

He nodded, collecting them again. "One for each of us, including Lisa."

"What's including Lisa?" Lisa asked, coming into the room. "Did I hear my name being bandied about?"

"The baseball game," Donna told her. Resigned, she put away the remaining bills. They'd keep. Somehow, they always did. "Frank got a ticket for you, too."

Lisa frowned dubiously. "I'll feel like a fifth wheel."

He wasn't going to let her beg off. This was a family outing. The key to Donna was her family. Besides, he rather liked the wisecracking woman and he knew that Donna would feel better if she came along. She'd probably like the Mormon Tabernacle Choir to come along, too, he mused, but he had to draw the line somewhere.

"Fifth wheels are very important," Frank told her. "I've always found them to be lifesavers myself."

"You do know how to turn a phrase." Lisa laughed, then looked at Donna. "This man is too good to get away. If you don't snatch him up, I will. Be ready in a few minutes," she promised, hurrying out of the room.

Donna pursed her lips, struggling with a wave of embarrassment. She leaned back in her chair. "Subtlety was never something that Lisa subscribed to."

He leaned his hip against her desk. "I find it refreshing."

Sure, because Lisa was on his side. "There's another word for it, but we won't go into that."

She sighed, then rose from her chair behind the desk. Who was she to fight the inevitable? Besides, she really did love baseball. She had a sneaking suspicion that Frank knew that. He'd probably pumped one of the boys to find out. No, on second thought, they had probably been more than eager to volunteer the information. Traitors.

If she was going to go to this game, she had better start things rolling.

"Well, if we're going, I might as well get ready." She stopped, halfway to the door, and looked at Frank. He had a great tan, but there was no sense in taking chances. "Did you put on any suntan lotion?"

"Suntan lotion?" He repeated the words innocently, tickled that she was beginning to worry about him. Definitely on the right track here, he thought.

"Suntan lotion," she reiterated impatiently as if she were talking to someone with limited mental capabilities. "You're going to be sitting out in the open, roasting for heaven only knows how long if for some reason we go into extra innings. I think you should put on lotion."

He draped an arm around her shoulders affectionately as they walked out of the room together. "Whatever you say."

"Yeah, right. As long as I say what you want to hear."

"Something like that," he agreed, then grew serious. He looked around and, for the moment, they were alone. He spoke quickly. "I just want you to know that, for what it's worth, I'm not like this with just anyone." Damn, he thought, it wasn't coming out right.

The man was incredibly good-looking. Wherever they'd gone yesterday, Donna had noticed women looking at him. And at her, enviously. "I do find that difficult to believe."

He grinned. "I'm outgoing, yes, but I don't kiss every woman I meet."

If he did, there would be a lot of women out there with no bones. "What's your criteria?"

She was kidding, but he wasn't. "I have to feel something." His eyes looked into hers. "When I look at you, Donna, I feel something. I'm not sure what—"

She didn't want him serious. "Hormones," she said flippantly.

He knew what she was doing and he wasn't about to let her get away with it. "There's that, of course, but it's just not that simple." She looked like a bird that wanted to take flight, but he had to make her understand. "I can't explain it, but I know that if I don't explore what's happening here, I'll regret it for the rest of my life." He looked at her and saw the skeptical expression on her face. She probably thought he was handing her a line. "Does that sound crazy to you?"

She wanted to say yes and drive him away, but she couldn't. She couldn't because there was some part of her that felt just as he did, some part of her that agreed with him.

"Maybe a little." She looked away. "Maybe not."

She'd said the words softly, but he'd heard her. "Do you feel it, too?"

Donna shrugged, stepping away from him. She couldn't concentrate when he was that close, couldn't form coherent thoughts.

"I don't know what I feel. Confused, mainly. I thought I had life all mapped out for myself. I was going to raise Taylor and Stephen and enjoy being there for my grandchildren. I wasn't going to fall in love again."

He was surprised at the admission. "Have you?"

It was a slip of the tongue. "No!" she snapped a little too firmly. "I was speaking figuratively. What I meant was—"

Closing her eyes, she gave up. If she protested, it would look as if she meant it. If she said nothing, it was as good as an admission. She lost either way.

"You'll find the suntan lotion in the medicine cabinet in the main bathroom. I'm going to see about getting some on the boys."

"I think Lisa's already taking care of that." He had seen her walk by with a bottle of lotion while Donna's back had been to the door.

She set her mouth hard, determined to get away. "Then I'm going to pack some sandwiches."

Frank held up his hand. "Too late. Angelina beat you to it."

"Angelina?" she repeated dumbly. "You asked Angelina to make sandwiches?" He nodded. "When did you get a chance to talk to her?"

"Just now."

It figured. Donna felt herself growing edgy. She was on a platform that was literally shrinking beneath her feet. "Then I'm going to change my clothes—" she eyed him, daring him to say something "—unless someone's already doing that."

"No," he conceded, and then a sensuous smile lifted his lips. "But I can help."

Donna braced a hand on his chest, immobilizing him. "You do, and it's the last thing you'll ever do."

He grinned. "Might be worth it. But, for the sake of the boys, I'll stay here. I wouldn't want them to see their mother on trial for manslaughter."

"Hold that thought," she advised as she walked away from him and to her bedroom.

When she reached her room, Donna closed the door and then leaned against it, vainly attempting to get her bearings. She was vacillating between excitement and fear. Between yearning and denying. It felt as if she were running for her life. But was her direction to or from?

Donna hadn't a clue.

Chapter Eight

The next six days were wrapped in a whirlwind. And in the center of it, calm if not calming, was Frank. Somehow—Donna wasn't quite sure how—he had become a part of their everyday lives. He turned up each evening for Taylor's music lessons. Sometimes he was even there when she returned from work. He was there to blend his life with theirs, to make suggestions about dinner as he looked over Angelina's shoulder in the kitchen, to listen to the boys rattle off the day's events in double-time, to talk things over with Lisa when she needed a sounding board, to help Stephen with his reading.

Everyone, Donna noted in amazement, seemed to accept this situation with no problem. Everyone else welcomed him into their lives as if they'd been waiting for him to appear all along. *She* was the only one having difficulty with it.

Frank did things with them. Simple things, such as taking them to a movie that *everyone* miraculously enjoyed. Or to an exclusive restaurant for dinner where even Taylor and Stephen called a cease-fire as they ate. He took them to the mall just to watch the people go by.

He infiltrated every tiny crack in Donna's life. If she let herself, she would easily begin to feel too comfortable, too secure.

That had been her mistake the first time. It couldn't go on.

She knew it, and yet each day she persuaded herself to let it linger just a tiny bit longer. Her safety net was that he was leaving at the end of his vacation. There was no actual harm in enjoying his presence just a little while longer, not if it wouldn't last. Besides, he was a better cook than either she or Lisa, and when Angelina was suddenly called away on a family emergency a few days before Donna had to leave for a three-day seminar on small businesses in San Diego, he proved invaluable.

Still, she shouldn't have let it go this far, she thought as she prepared to take the laundry basket out to the car. Somehow, things had managed to get away from her. They had started escaping the moment she'd laid eyes on him, she mused.

Donna looked down ruefully at the basket. If things hadn't gotten so out of hand, she wouldn't have forgotten to call the washing-machine repairman. Now the boys were out of underwear, and instead of packing for her trip tomorrow, she was going to have to cart off the laundry to the nearest Laundromat, some five miles away.

A loud noise from the family room startled her. Laundry basket clutched in her hands, she hurried to see what had happened.

When she entered the room, Stephen was standing by the sofa, his lower lip thrust out in a sulky pout. At his red sneakered feet lay his reader, sprawled out like a lackey in obvious disfavor, begging for forgiveness.

Stephen didn't notice that his mother was in the room. His attention was focused on the offending book. "I'll never get this. I'll never learn how to read. Never." He swung his foot, about to kick the book, then thought better of it. He knew that, temper or no temper, he'd never get away with damaging a book. His mother had very strict rules about things like that.

He hadn't so much as glanced her way, but Donna knew Frank saw her. Feeling foolish, standing there, clutching a laundry basket, she set it down.

"Sure you will. You know why?" Frank asked patiently as he picked up the book from the floor and pretended to dust it off.

Stephen shook his head, his straight hair shimmying around his head. "No, why?"

Frank rose. He looked down into the petulant face. "Because you're smart."

The lower lip retracted, but Stephen's expression remained sullen and unconvinced. "If I was smart, I'd know how to read, like you and Mommy." He jerked a disgusted thumb toward his brother on the sofa. "Even Taylor knows how to read."

Frank placed a wide, comforting hand on the small shoulders. "Yes, but we all had to learn how once upon a time."

Stephen looked up at Frank uncertainly. Surprise raised the dark crescents above his eyes high on his forehead, hiding them beneath his unruly hair. "You did?"

"Sure." Unable to resist, Frank tousled the boy's hair. "What do you think, we were born reading?"

Stephen raised his shoulders and then let them drop in an exaggerated motion. "When I was born, you were all reading."

Taylor let out a mocking hoot. "A lot you know, Step-On. I learned how to read in the first grade." A sickly child, Taylor had remained home with Donna until he went to first grade.

A spark lit Stephen's eyes. "Hey, I'm just in kindergarten."

"See that?" Frank held the reader out to Stephen as if it represented a goal to be attained. "You'll learn how to do something sooner than Taylor did."

The grin that burst forth on Stephen's face threatened to split it in half. Taylor decided it was time to leave the room.

"Yeah!" Stephen almost snatched the reader from Frank and clutched it to his small, yellow T-shirt-clad chest.

Frank successfully swallowed his laugh. "Why don't you take a break for a little while and then I'll help you some more?"

Stephen raised his head high, like a little prince leaving the room where his loyal subjects were gathered. "I think I'll go to the living room and do some reading." He ran off, still holding the reader.

Donna couldn't help the admiration that rose to her eyes as she watched the exchange. "Nice piece of child psychology."

Frank shoved his hands into his back pockets and crossed to her. "*People* psychology," he corrected. "Works every time."

He was shrugging it off as if it were nothing. Still, as a veteran of continual warfare between her sons, whether it was over chores or studies, or just about getting along with each other for ten minutes at a time, this display of calm reasoning and its reception was pretty amazing to her. Especially since the man was a bachelor. "How did you manage to become so patient with kids?"

He shrugged. "Easy. I used to be one myself." His glance ran over her, making her feel warm and definitely unchildlike. "How about you?"

She nodded as she bent to pick up the basket again. "Sure. A million years ago."

He looked down at the laundry. "Running away from home?"

Donna laughed. "Just as far as the Laundromat."

"Don't you have a washing machine?" He was certain that he had seen one through the open garage door.

"Yes," she said cryptically. "Now ask me if I have a 'functioning' washing machine."

He laughed as he took the basket from her and followed her out of the family room. "Obviously not. What's wrong with it?"

"Nothing a bullet between the spin and rinse cycle couldn't fix. It won't empty out the water." She looked at him as they entered the hall. "I was supposed to call the repairman earlier this week, but you got me so distracted, I forgot all about it.''

He leaned the basket on his hip and grinned. ''I did, did I?''

There was no sense in hiding the truth. Besides, there was such a thing as giving the devil his due, no matter what Lisa said about guardian angels. ''Yes.''

Progress. If the boys hadn't been home, he would have tried his hand at progressing a little further. He had a feeling about this. A good feeling. He could wait. ''I guess, then, it's my fault.''

''In a way,'' she admitted. Then she added, ''In a very large way.'' She reached for the basket, but Frank merely shifted it so he was holding the basket with both hands.

''Let me take a look at it.''

She cocked her head, looking at him dubiously. ''You fix washing machines on the side?''

A machine was a machine, and machines had always fascinated him. Even as a child he'd liked to take things apart and put them back together.

''I tinker,'' he replied tentatively. ''Who knows? Maybe I'll get lucky and it's just something simple.''

She already knew him well enough to know that he wasn't about to give up easily. She motioned him to follow her. ''C'mon.''

Leading the way, she walked into the two-car garage. Her own was parked in the driveway, giving them room to move about the semicluttered space. She waved a disparaging hand at the beige machine that stood huddled next to the dryer. It was just the slightest bit askew.

''There's the beast. I spent a whole hour bailing it out on Tuesday. I had to finish the laundry by hand.''

He set the basket down on the floor. ''Knew you had pioneer stock in you.''

She frowned. ''What I had was chapped hands when I finished.''

He took one hand in both of his and stroked it. ''Not that I noticed.''

"Never mind." She pulled her hand away. "Do you really think you can do anything with it?"

She'd gone from doubting to believing. He liked that. Frank rested his hands on the lid as he studied the machine thoughtfully for a moment.

Donna arched a brow. "Planning to lay hands on it and heal it?"

He smiled vaguely, ignoring her sarcasm. "It'll probably take a little more than that." He raised the lid and looked in. It smelled dank and musty, as if she hadn't managed to bail out all the water. "Were you missing something in the laundry?"

"What?"

Frank let the lid drop again. "When you folded the laundry, did you notice that an article of clothing was missing?"

She shook her head, then explained before he thought she meant no. "I didn't fold the laundry. Angelina did. She didn't mention anything, but she probably wouldn't have noticed unless she had an extra sock on her hands."

He nodded, weighing the odds. "It's worth a look." He crouched down and tilted the machine back to ascertain where the screws had been placed. He looked at Donna over his shoulder. "Got a screwdriver?"

Just how sheltered did he think she was? "Of course I've got a screwdriver. We're not entirely helpless here, you know."

"Never said you were," he answered easily. "The screwdriver?"

She flushed. Here he was helping, and she was jumping down his throat. *Jumping*—that was the word for it all right. She felt jumpy, but that was entirely because of him.

There was a toolbox on one of the shelves that lined the left wall of the garage. She opened the dusty lid and rummaged through the clutter. There were tools in there she had no idea how to use, pointy things that looked more like something someone would duel with than use to fix a machine. They'd belonged to Tony. This had been his domain, not hers. But she located what he wanted.

She turned, holding two screwdrivers in her hand. "Flat or Phillips?"

"Phillips." He glanced along the border of the washing machine and saw another set of screws. "On second thought, bring both."

She handed him the tools. Frank set the Phillips head aside for the time being. Donna crouched down beside him and looked over his shoulder, trying to keep out of the way. He pushed the machine back again, rocking it on its rear coasters.

"What are you going to do?"

He was already working on the second screw. Methodically, he set each screw down in precise order. "Look around. A lot of times, these things are very simple to repair."

She felt guilty. He wouldn't be doing this if she hadn't told him it was his fault that she forgot to call the repairman.

"Don't go through any trouble." Donna rose to her feet and glanced at the basket in the corner. Getting the laundry done was going to eat into time she couldn't really spare, but so be it. "I can just pop over to the Laundromat and—"

From his position on the floor, he caught her hand and held her in place. "Let me satisfy my male pride."

She sighed and relented. If he fixed it, it *would* be a savings, both in time and money. If he didn't, she'd be even further behind than she was now, but she let him continue.

"As long as it's on the washing machine and not me."

He grinned as he continued working. His hands were on the machine, but his mind was on the woman standing behind him whose scent was getting under his skin. As usual. "Why, do I loosen your bolts, Donna?"

"Bolts, screws and wing nuts." She ticked each off on her fingers.

He looked over his shoulder, wondering if she was being sarcastic. Her expression told him she wasn't. "I had no idea."

"Neither did I." Donna shoved her hands into her front pockets. She'd never thought that things could evolve to this state for her. Until they did. And at such a breathtaking rate, too. She couldn't begin to make heads or tails out of it, and it made her even more nervous.

Donna tried to get her mind back on the defunct washing machine. She watched as Frank took off the front piece of metal sheeting. Rising, he separated the two large tubs inside.

"Can you put that back together again?" she asked dubiously.

"With my eyes shut. But it helps if I keep them open." He spared her a glance. "I like to see what my hands are doing."

A flash of warmth zoomed over her before it disappeared again. "I bet you do."

"Ah, here's your problem." Like a hunter holding up the pelt of an animal he had bagged, Frank held up what had once been a very lacy bra. It was now mangled and discolored. "I think the machine was trying it on for size."

With a flush of embarrassment, Donna took the bra away from him and stuffed it into her back pocket.

"Yours?" he asked innocently.

As if he hadn't already figured that out. "Yes, mine. I'd wondered where it had gotten to." She had looked for it just this morning, she realized. Donna felt his eyes on her.

"Does it have a mate?" She looked at him quizzically. "A twin," he prodded. "One that looks just like it?" His grin was wide, guileless, and it upended her stomach altogether. "I'd like to see what it looked like before the machine mauled it." Frank replaced the metal cover, then crouched down to replace the screws. He grinned boyishly. "Preferably filled out."

The mere thought of it had his palms damp. Another adolescent reaction. No, he amended. He'd never felt this sort of anticipation as an adolescent. She had his number and was slowly turning him inside out without having done a thing.

When she laughed, he looked up. "I could put it on the cat," Donna volunteered.

"That wasn't quite what I had in mind." He tilted the machine back to tighten the screws.

Donna watched, fascinated, as the muscles on his forearm strained while he balanced the machine and told herself she wasn't affected. But her mouth was dry. "I know what you have in mind and it's not going to happen."

He rose. Placing the screwdrivers on the washing machine, he brushed his hands off on the back of his jeans. "I've learned *never* to say never. A few weeks ago, if anyone would have asked me if I was ever going to fix a washing machine in Seattle for a beautiful woman who all but took my breath away, I would have said never. And, see?" He spread his hands wide. "I just did."

She looked at the machine skeptically. "We don't know that yet."

He leaned a hip against the dryer, his eyes caressing her. "I'm willing to stake my reputation on it."

Donna was unaware of licking her dry lips, but Frank wasn't. "That would be your world-famous reputation as a washing-machine repairman?"

He grinned again, wanting to touch her. He was just barely managing to rein himself in. "That and other things." His eyes coaxed her. "C'mon Donna, take a chance. What have you got to lose?"

She pressed her lips together, her eyes on his, her heart in her throat. They weren't talking about washing machines any longer. "More than laundry."

"Maybe not even that." Frank set the dials on the machine and then deposited her laundry. Underwear rained in with shirts and dirty denim shorts.

When he pulled out the dial to start the wash, she laid her hand over his. "Hold it, you haven't presorted them yet."

Frank had never bothered separating fabrics. "I always do everything together. My clothes seem to hold up pretty well."

"Pure luck." She pushed the dial in, stopping the flow of water. "You're not supposed to mix them."

"I find mixing a lot of fun." Frank fitted his hands comfortably around her waist, then drew her to him. Close. She didn't resist, couldn't resist.

It pleased him.

Frank touched his lips to hers and heard her sigh softly beneath them.

"You're doing it again."

"What?" he asked as he kissed her once, twice, three times, losing a little more of himself each time. "What am I doing again?"

Donna fought to keep her eyes from closing, from giving in to urges that tugged at her, from caring about him. "Scrambling my brain."

Frank feathered his hand over her temples. "You don't need it."

She was sinking, sinking fast. Donna dug her fingers into his arms, as if that would keep her from going under. "What? You'll do the thinking for the both of us?"

Gently his lips whispered along her face, wreathing it in kisses so soft, she wanted to cry. He could feel her trembling.

"I wasn't planning on it. I wasn't planning on thinking at all." He wound his fingers in her hair, loving the feel of it. Loving her. He'd always suspected that when love happened, *if* it happened, it would come quickly. But he had never expected to be surfing along the rim of a lightning bolt.

He was now.

Frank brought his mouth back to hers, and this time, when she opened her lips in silent invitation, he was instantly lost, instantly, painfully, aroused.

Wanting had never hurt like this before.

He wasn't certain how much longer he could maintain his emotions on a choke chain.

Because she was safe here, standing in the middle of the garage where anyone could walk in and find them at any moment, Donna allowed herself the wanton pleasure of savoring, of feeling. Of accepting the wild rush Frank created within her and hanging on, white-knuckled, for the ride.

She moaned as his mouth left hers, then grazed her chin and pressed a kiss so very softly to her throat. She might even have said his name—she wasn't certain. It was throbbing in her brain, in time to the yearning that sprang forth.

She wasn't certain of anything at all except that she loved what he did to her.

"Still want to separate the whites from the brights?" he asked.

Her body leaning into his, Donna reached over and pulled the dial out on the washing machine. Water began to pour into the machine. Her mouth, inches from his, curved. "Let 'er ride."

Frank kissed her again and effectively melted every remaining bone in her body within three seconds.

The door between the house and the garage flew open with a bang. "Mom, don't forget I need my blue shirt for assembly tomorrow—"

One foot into the garage, Taylor came to a skidding halt. His face was a mask of surprise and then anger as he looked accusingly from Frank to Donna. The next moment, he spun on his heel and fled.

"Taylor!" Donna cried. Oh, God, what had she done? She hadn't prepared either of her sons for the possibility of her seeing another man. How could she? She hadn't even prepared herself for it. "Taylor, you don't—"

Frantic, Donna started to go after him. Frank stopped her.

"No, let me."

She looked at Frank, upset with him, more upset with herself. Why had she been so weak? "It's because of you that he ran off."

They both knew he didn't deserve that, but for now he let the accusation go. "Then I should be the one to talk to him."

He left her standing there, feeling helpless and frustrated. And so damn confused, she could scream.

The washing machine churned along relentlessly in the background.

Frank found Taylor in his room. As he entered, the boy was jamming the guitar into the closet. He slammed the door on it, muttering under his breath.

It would have been safer to leave him alone. Safer and more cowardly. Frank crossed to the boy as the latter threw himself, facedown, on Stephen's bed. "Giving up?"

"Go away." His voice was muffled against the Seattle Mariners pattern on the comforter.

Frank sat down on the edge of the bed. He placed his hand on the boy's shoulder. Taylor jerked away and kept his face buried.

"I'm not going to do that, Taylor," Frank said quietly. "So why don't you tell me why you're shoving the guitar away? You were doing very well."

Taylor raised himself up on his forearms. When he spoke, it was to the wall. "It was a dumb idea."

"To improve yourself? I don't think so. I think it's an admirable, peaceful way to show those guys that you're every bit as good as they are." He paused. "Maybe, in some cases, better."

Taylor sat up and turned around to look at Frank. His chin went up just the way Frank had seen Donna's rise up when she felt challenged. "What do you care? You're not my father."

"No, I'm not," Frank agreed. "But I don't have to be your father to care." He placed his hand on the boy's slim shoulder again and this time, Taylor didn't pull away. "I do, Taylor." He spoke very quietly, making the words all the more important. "I care very much. About you, your brother, your Aunt Lisa."

Taylor cocked his head, watching Frank's expression. "And my mom?" he challenged.

"Oh, yes." Frank nodded and smiled. The smile took in Taylor. "I really do care for your mom." And it felt good to say it out loud. Good, and scary at the same time. "Does it make you uneasy?"

Taylor shrugged, unable to deal with his emotions. "Kinda."

"I'll tell you a secret." Frank bent closer to the boy. "It kind of makes me uneasy, too."

Taylor looked at him, surprised. "Why?"

"Because I've never felt like this about anyone before. But it shouldn't make *you* uneasy. What happens between your mother and me doesn't affect the way she feels about you and your brother. Or the way she felt about your father." He could see the inner struggle that was going on in the boy's eyes. Frank placed his arm around Taylor and drew him closer. "Let me put it this way. What's your favorite ice cream, Taylor?"

Frank could feel the suspicion completely drain from the boy. "That's easy. Fudge ripple."

"Great choice. Now let's say that they suddenly stopped making fudge ripple. Fudge ripple was never going to be made again." He eyed Taylor. "Does that mean that you'd never eat any other flavor of ice cream again, not even to sample it?"

Taylor laughed, dismissing the suggestion as stupid. "No, of course not." He stopped and looked at Frank, mulling over what Frank had just said. "Are you another flavor of ice cream?"

"I certainly hope so."

Taylor sighed, then nodded in his most manly fashion. "I guess I can live with that."

"That's all I ask." Frank rose from the bunk bed and crossed to the closet. When he opened the door, the guitar fell at his feet. Picking it up, he walked over to Taylor with it. "Except that you practice with your guitar." He held the instrument out to Taylor.

Taylor took the guitar and tucked it against his chest, placing his fingers on the frets the way Frank had showed him. "Okay. Will you listen?"

Frank leaned his hip against the small desk. "Sure."

Taylor began to play. His fingering was much more assured and the notes sounded sweet.

Donna leaned against the wall outside Taylor's room and blinked back tears. Unable to just sit back and let Frank handle what she deemed a family affair, she had hurried to Taylor's room. And been in time to hear the exchange between her son and Frank.

He was winning everyone over, Donna thought. Small wonder. He had already won her over, at least the part of her that was reasonable.

Emotionally, she still hung back. Would continue to hang back. It involved a matter of survival.

She could never again go through what she had when Tony died. She'd loved Tony with all her heart and he had left her with only shards to hold on to. Shards of a heart, and shards of a life, to put back together.

And guilt.

There had been a horrid, horrid sense of guilt haunting her since his death. Guilt that held her prisoner in the wee hours of the night. Guilt that held her prisoner even now. Tony had taken his own life, he'd stated in the note he'd left for her, because he couldn't face her.

That made it her fault.

He had killed himself and it was her fault. That obligated her to him and shackled her emotions. Permanently. She wasn't free to ever love again, even if she could.

Donna wiped away the tears that had formed as she walked away. She had things to do and a trip to prepare for. She had no time to dwell on the past. Or a future that couldn't be allowed to happen.

Chapter Nine

She was gone for a total of three days. During that time, Donna felt as if her soul were locked away somewhere, restless, unable to find a place for itself. And it all had to do with Frank.

It had been almost two weeks since they'd met. Two weeks. Far too little time to feel the way she did.

Yet she did.

No matter how much she tried, how hard she ran, her footing kept slipping and she continued to slide toward something she was far too afraid of.

Barely two weeks. Not enough time to know.

More than enough time to feel.

Donna tried to get a grip on her emotions as she drove home from the airport. In all probability, Frank might not even be there when she arrived home. And she had given him no reason to believe that she wanted him there.

None save when she'd kissed him goodbye, she thought, bringing her car to a skidding stop at a red light a mile away from her house.

Damn, she had to keep her mind on the road, she upbraided herself.

But as soon as she put her foot back on the accelerator, her mind drifted to Frank. She had remained in his arms perhaps a moment too long, let her lips linger on his an instant too much. And maybe she had even sighed when she had stepped back.

She'd said her goodbyes to him before she'd left for her flight and had made it sound final. But there had been nothing final in her kiss.

Or in his.

All moot, she told herself. There was no point in analyzing her departure. The man was probably gone. She tried to convince herself of that as she continued the drive home. Tried to convince herself of the fact that she didn't mind that he was gone.

She had almost succeeded by the time she pulled up in the driveway.

Bracing her shoulders, Donna forced a cheery smile to her face as she unlocked her front door. The foyer was deserted. "Hey, where is everyone? I'm home!"

Within a moment, she was in the middle of a four-armed embrace as Taylor and Stephen flanked her on two sides.

"Hey, nice to be missed," she said, laughing, then looked down at their faces.

There was something wrong, she thought suddenly. Instincts that had no logical foundation to them told her that Stephen was holding on to her a little tighter than he should have and that there was concern in Taylor's eyes, a wariness she wasn't quite sure how to describe. She only knew it was unusual.

Maybe she was just overreacting. "What's up, men?"

She sensed him a moment before she looked up. Frank was standing there, in the doorway of the living room, giving her a moment of privacy with her children.

Donna felt her heart lurch against her rib cage, as if it were a bird suddenly set free from its cage. *He hadn't left.* She tried to stifle the feeling of happiness that was attempting to break through. Uncertainty's steely fingers managed to hold it back at the last moment.

Donna rested a hand on Taylor's shoulder, anchoring herself to something solid. Something that was a given in her life. "I thought you'd be gone by now."

One dark, velvety brow arched as Frank studied her.

He searched her eyes, looking for the truth. Did she really want him to leave? Their parting had left things up in the air, but he had believed that neither one of them wanted things to end that abruptly. He knew he didn't. This was a maze he was in, an emotional maze. He was still feeling his way around, trying to make sense of it all. Trying to make sense out of the new emotions he was experiencing and the great intensity with which he wanted her in his life.

He crossed to her. The children stood between them. "Afraid not. There have been some extenuating circumstances."

Now what did he meant by that? She looked from Frank's face to her sons'.

"He's living here, now," Stephen volunteered.

Donna realized that her mouth had dropped open. "What?"

"Yeah!" It was obvious that Stephen, at least, was very happy about the arrangement. "He's sleeping in Aunt Lisa's room."

Moving toward the sofa in a daze, Donna slowly lowered herself onto it. This was too much. Her eyes narrowed as her head spun in disbelief. Lisa and Frank? Lisa? The thought of Frank being with another woman brought a stabbing sensation with it. Donna felt as if a sword had been sunk deep into her stomach.

Or her heart.

She couldn't have it both ways, she taunted herself, and now she didn't have it any way at all.

But with Lisa?

Donna raised her eyes to Frank's. Her tone was bitter. "Move fast, don't you?"

Stephen had blurted out the words before Frank had had the opportunity to prepare Donna for the news. Obviously, things never went according to plan with children around. "It's not what you think."

She rose to her feet again, incensed. Just what kind of a fool did he take her for? "I leave for three days and you move into my sister-in-law's room. And with the children here." How could he? How could he do that with her sons in the house? How could Lisa? "What am I supposed to think?"

Was she jealous? he wondered. The indignation that painted her cheeks in bright red hues wasn't just about Lisa's honor. Though he didn't care for her yelling at him, he certainly did enjoy the reason behind it.

Frank's voice was maddeningly calm as he answered, "What you're supposed to think is that I was taking care of your sons."

"What?" This wasn't making any sense. She looked around. "Where *is* Lisa?"

She was probably hiding, too ashamed to face her, Donna thought. But she couldn't blame Lisa. She could, and did, however, blame Frank. This was all his fault. *Everything* was all his fault. If he hadn't come on the scene, looking the way he did, acting the way he did, none of this would be happening. She wouldn't have spent a miserable three days in San Diego, searching her soul for an answer and coming up empty while a lecture she had paid good money for dragged on at the front of the seminar hall.

"Aunt Lisa's in the hospital," Taylor told her.

"What?" Donna whispered. Horror etched itself into her features. So that was what she'd felt when she walked in. That was what was wrong. Stunned, she turned on Frank. "What did you do to her?"

The smile on his lips didn't reach his eyes. "Thanks for the vote of confidence," he said evenly, but Donna could have sworn she heard a note of hurt in it.

Donna held her head, wishing back the words. They had come out all wrong. Everything was getting so confused.

"I didn't mean that the way it sounded. *Why* is Lisa in the hospital and *why* are you living here?" She raised her hand as Stephen opened his mouth, obviously ready to launch into an animated explanation. "Slowly," she begged. "From the top."

"I came over yesterday evening to help Taylor with his guitar lesson—" Frank began.

The fact that he was still working with Taylor, even when she wasn't around, really astonished her. Was he altruistic after all? She had no idea what to make of the man.

"And I'm really good, Mom," Taylor interjected eagerly, his face bursting with confidence. "I can play the song straight through now. Frank's teaching me a couple more. Wanna hear?" He was already halfway across the room, rushing to fetch his guitar.

"Later." Donna stopped Taylor in middash. "Soon, I promise. First I want to hear what happened to Aunt Lisa." She turned toward Frank. "Go on."

"I noticed that she looked a little pale at dinner and that she hadn't eaten much. Her appetite had been fading the last couple of days."

God, he was so entrenched in their lives, he knew their eating patterns, she thought.

"I asked her if anything was wrong. That was when she told me she had this persistent pain in her right side." Frank pressed his hand to the spot to illustrate. "She tried to laugh it off, but I could see she was really in pain. I hardly had to touch it before she was wincing."

Donna said the first thing that occurred to her. "Appendicitis?"

"A first-class case." Frank nodded. "I told her that it was nothing she wanted to take chances with. I grabbed the boys and we took her to the emergency room."

Donna noticed that Frank used the word *we* in his narrative and that both boys puffed up their chests when he did. He was good at this, she couldn't help thinking. Good at winning everyone over and keeping them on his side.

"Just in time, too," he continued. "Her appendix ruptured while she was on the operating table."

Donna covered her mouth with her fingertips, smothering a gasp as she attempted to get a grip on her nerves. She let out a long breath. "I just talked to her yesterday morning. She said everything was fine."

Frank lifted a shoulder and let it drop. "You know Lisa. She doesn't like to complain."

Donna stared at Frank. He was talking as if he'd known Lisa for years instead of just under two weeks. Could a man get so entangled in a family's life in such a short amount of time? Could *she* get that entangled with a man in such a short amount of time? With Tony, the process had been slow, like a tapestry that was being patiently woven. They'd grown up together and fallen in love by degrees. None of this wham, right-between-the-eyes chemistry.

What was sizzling between Frank and her had come into existence with the speed of light. Would it leave just as fast?

And what was she doing, analyzing hormonal reactions when her sister-in-law lay in a hospital bed, narrowly having escaped death?

Donna felt as if her brain were in a frying pan, being systematically scrambled.

"Angelina is still away. She won't be back for another few days," Frank was saying. "There wasn't anyone else to stay with the boys until you returned." It didn't bear explaining, but he did, anyway. "So I spent the night in Lisa's room." Because Stephen gave him a wide, toothy grin, Frank couldn't resist tousling his hair. He looked at Donna over the boy's head. "That's the whole story. Everything's under control."

Embarrassed now about the conclusion she had leapt to, especially since he had been so good about everything, she flushed.

"It's been a rough day, Frank. I'm sorry. I didn't mean to snap at you. I thought that you…" Her voice trailed off.

"I know what you thought."

And he looked pretty smug about it, she noted. She had really put her foot into it this time.

"He made us breakfast and got us to school in time and everything," Stephen told her. The look on his face said that he'd been surprised, but that he forgave Frank for making him go to school. "I thought maybe we could stay home on account of Aunt Lisa being sick, but Frank said that it was important not to miss any classes."

Donna draped her arm around the boy and hugged him to her. Never a dull moment. "Frank's right."

"About a lot of things," Frank interjected, looking at her pointedly.

Donna raised her chin, determined to hang on to the shred of pride she had left to her. "About *most* things." She blew out a breath. This had been some homecoming. "What hospital is she in?"

"St. Cecilia's." Frank took a step toward her and Stephen shuffled out of the way. "I'll drive you," he offered. "I'm getting pretty good at finding my way around here, although I have to admit that I really like the streets in Wilmington Falls better. A traffic jam over there is when two cars meet simultaneously at a stop sign and can't decide who has the right of way."

"What's simul-simul—that word?" Stephen asked.

Frank laughed. The boy had a mind like a sponge, always looking for another spill to absorb. "It means at the same time."

"Like having you and Mom here now?"

Frank inclined his head, willing to agree. "Something like that."

She felt exhausted. Donna had sat through the last tedious lecture this morning and then had spent four hours in the air, piloting one of her own four-seaters. She'd spent half an hour catching up at the office before heading home. There had been a jackknifed truck on the expressway. The twenty-minute ride home had taken her an hour. "Right now, the thought of living somewhere with no traffic jams sounds heavenly."

Frank arched a brow. "How about later?"

Donna blinked. Had she missed something? "What?"

"How would living somewhere like that sound a week from now? Or a month?"

Donna looked at him warily, belatedly realizing her mistake. "What are you saying?"

He smoothed the crease in her brow with his thumb. "What do you think I'm saying?"

She didn't want to discuss it now, not in front of Taylor and Stephen. She didn't know how she felt anymore. Either way seemed wrong. "Let's go see Lisa."

Frank bowed low at the waist. "Your wish is my command."

Donna gave a skeptical laugh. "If that were true—"

"What?" His mesmerizing green eyes held hers. "If it were true, what?"

She shook her head. She had been about to say, "then you'd leave me alone," but it seemed coldly ungrateful of her. And it wasn't what she meant. Not really. Oh, God, she just didn't want to feel torn anymore.

"Never mind."

Frank turned toward Taylor and Stephen. Taylor gave him a knowing wink. The boy was older than he appeared, Frank decided. "Get in the car, boys. We'll be right there."

Donna was still amazed at the way her sons obeyed Frank without question. Cheerfully. Instantly. The novelty, as he had pointed out, should have worn off by now. It hadn't. Instead, like colors that bled into a fabric, their reaction to him only became more ingrained.

But he was leaving, she reminded herself. It was only a matter of time before he wouldn't be here any longer. There was no sense in getting attached.

No sense at all.

Emotional attachment had very little to do with sense, she decided as she watched her sons hurry off to the garage.

Her breath caught as Frank drew her into his arms. "I haven't said hello yet."

She was going to contradict him, but her words died quickly, unexpressed, the moment he touched his lips to hers.

The kiss flowered, deepened. It effectively wiped away all thoughts from her mind. All thoughts, all arguments, all indecisions. It wiped out everything except the desire to have him here with her.

All of the time.

Each time he kissed her, the fuse was a little shorter, the detonation a little hotter. She could almost feel her skin sizzling as he pressed her against him. Or was that her, pressing against him? She didn't know. Whichever way it was, she was melting, and a sense of urgency vibrated all through her.

God, she had missed him. Missed him without wanting to. Missed him even though she knew it was bad for her to feel this way. It would only lead her down a road she had no intentions of going.

She'd been there before. And returned painfully alone.

But the path had never been so bright, her yearning never so great.

His arms wrapped around her, Frank stroked her hair, her shoulders, contenting himself with bits and pieces, a nibble when he wanted to devour, a taste when he wanted to swallow. The reins of the situation were all in her hands. Things would only progress if she wanted them to.

But it wasn't easy for him.

Like a runner who had pushed too hard, Donna found that she couldn't catch her breath as she drew her mouth from his. Waiting for her pulse to steady, she leaned her head against his. Her whole body vibrated from wanting him. She was grateful that her sons were so close by. Otherwise, she would have been tempted to make a fatal mistake and give the rest of her heart to him. Give the rest of herself to him, body and soul.

"Hello," he murmured.

"Hello," she breathed, her mouth slowly curving as she looked up into his eyes.

Frank threaded his fingers through hers. "Let's go. The boys are waiting for us."

Donna's heart tightened in sympathy when she slowly opened the hospital room door. Lisa looked exceptionally pale, her hair spread out on the pillow like tarnished gold. There were two bottles on separate intravenous racks next to her bed, each feeding something into her arms via long, cream-colored tubes. Lisa's eyes were closed when they filed into the single-care unit. Donna was tempted just to ease out of the room again and let Lisa continue sleeping.

"Aunt Lisa, we're here," Stephen announced loudly, rushing in front of Taylor.

"Shh." Donna laid a warning finger against her lips for the boy's benefit. "She's sleeping."

"No, she's not," Lisa contradicted as she slowly opened her eyes, a crack at a time. They felt gritty and weighted down. "I was just dreaming about all of you." Smiling weakly, she opened her arms to her nephews, then realized that she was tethered. She looked from one bottle to the other, resigned, and dropped her arms. "So, how are my guys getting along without me?"

"Great," Stephen proclaimed. He would have scrambled onto her bed and probably onto her, if Frank hadn't placed a hand on his shoulder, gently holding him in place.

"What Step-On means—" Taylor gave his brother a glare "—is that we miss you."

"Yeah," Stephen chimed in, not to be outdone, "we miss you. Frank gave us cheese melts for breakfast."

"You were out of cereal," he explained to Donna, who had given him a quizzical look. He thought it safer to turn his attention to Lisa. He brushed the tips of his fingers against hers. "How are you feeling?"

Lisa tried to shrug, and then thought better of it. "I've been better," she confided philosophically. Then a wicked, if somewhat weak, grin managed to emerge. "The nursing staff leaves something to be desired."

St. Cecilia's had a great reputation. Donna was surprised at Lisa's complaint. "They're not treating you right?" She was prepared to speak to the head nurse, prodded in part by her guilt at having wronged Lisa when she'd coupled her with Frank.

"Oh, they've been very kind and all, but I keep waiting for them to send in a strapping, six-foot hunk to give me a back rub. All I get are kindly-looking grandmothers in squeaky shoes." She smiled at Frank. "It's not fair."

Lisa turned her head to look at Donna. Her sister-in-law's face was creased with concern. As if she didn't have enough to worry about, Lisa thought. "Sorry about this, Donna."

"You didn't exactly engineer a ruptured appendix, Lisa."
Donna squeezed her hand, thinking of what might have
been. "Are you all right?"

"Sure." Lisa's eyes shifted to look at Frank. "Your guy
got me here just in time."

It was on the tip of Donna's tongue to deny the term. He
wasn't her guy. He wasn't anything to her. No, she amended
silently, that would have been a lie.

"He's...pretty handy to have around," Donna conceded. She felt his hand on her shoulder and could almost
feel his pleasure.

Frank laughed. "Coming from you, I'll take that as a
huge compliment."

Lisa's eyes widened as she suddenly remembered. "Did
you—?"

He was way ahead of her. "I called your office first thing
this morning." He shifted so that she could see him without having to turn her head. "Mr. Rice sounded very concerned. He said he'd send the proper disability insurance
papers around for you to fill out. He told me to tell you that
he'd have Simon and Walker handle your case load until
you're well enough to return."

Lisa blew out a breath, relieved. "You're a saint, Frank."

He shook his head, feigning modesty. "Nah, just your
ordinary, run-of-the-mill superhero." He winked at her.
Then, because he had spent so much time in the company of
his mother and sister, he was able to sense that Donna and
Lisa wanted some time alone.

"Well, I'll leave you two to talk a little. C'mon, guys."
With his hand in his pocket, he jingled his change, then
placed a hand on either boy's shoulder. "Let's see if we can
find a full vending machine somewhere."

"I don't want you to eat too much candy," Donna called
after them. She knew the plea fell on deaf ears. Three sets
to be exact. She turned back to Lisa as the door whispered
shut again. "How are you, really?"

"It hurts like hell, but it could have been a lot worse."
Lisa smiled ruefully. "I would not be hurting at all right
now if he hadn't bullied me into coming to the hospital. I

was going to wait it out at home." She shuddered when she thought of the consequences to that. "You know how I hate going to doctors."

Donna covered Lisa's hand with her own as best she could. "I know."

Whatever Donna said to the contrary, a part of Lisa felt that there was a guardian angel looking over their collective shoulders.

"Donna, I don't know what I would have done without Frank. By the time I arrived at the hospital, I was too sick to even move. He took over everything. Me, the boys. He's a godsend, Donna. Do you know he carried me out of the car?" She smiled at the memory of it. "I only wish I'd been in some kind of condition to enjoy it. What I do remember is a great deal of pain and the boys being really frightened. He calmed them down, bullied the E.R. receptionist into letting me go in first and kept everything together for us. I didn't even have to ask him to take the boys. He just did. He has this way about him."

Donna remembered the way Frank had taken charge on the airplane with Rosemary. How gentle he had been with the pregnant woman, calming her fears and talking her through the delivery. And how, when it was all over and any obligation he might have had was gone, he had called Rosemary's husband to let him know what was happening. Frank didn't *have* to do any of that for Rosemary.

Or for her own family, Donna thought, looking at Lisa.

There was no arguing with the fact that the man was pretty terrific.

So what was stopping her from grabbing him and holding on for all she was worth? Fear, nothing but white-hot fear.

"I saw the doctor this morning," Lisa was saying to her, and Donna felt ashamed that she had allowed her mental warfare to make her drift off. "He said I should be home in about three or four days. Frank said he'd help you bring me home."

That meant he intended on staying longer. Donna shook her head. "I don't understand. When I first met him, he said he was only staying a week. That was almost two weeks ago."

Lisa smiled. Why was Donna fighting this so hard? "Maybe he's found something that makes him want to stay."

"Temporary. It's all only temporary," Donna reminded her a little too fiercely.

"So? Find a way to make it permanent." Donna's expression turned somber and she began to move away. Lisa grabbed her hand and held onto it, despite the tubes. "I see the way he looks at you." Donna began to retort, but Lisa wouldn't let her. "And the way you look at him."

"Chemistry, Lisa. I already told you that." She'd tried hard to hold on to that excuse, but even now her grasp was slipping.

Weak or not, Lisa wasn't buying it. She had eyes. "Chemistry is what happens when you fall for some empty-headed, good-looking stud who's not worth a damn. This guy is pure gold—fourteen carat."

She dared Donna to deny it. They'd both had enough evidence to see she was right.

"I—" Donna started to protest, but what was there to protest? She agreed with Lisa's assessment. The man was wonderful. And when he kissed her, liquefaction set in. "Yes, I know."

"So?"

Donna began to pace again, as if somehow, if she walked far enough, she could outdistance her feelings. Or at least arrive at some kind of logic that would see her through this. "So old feelings don't go away so quickly."

"Old feelings?" Lisa was struggling to understand why a bright woman like Donna would throw away a gift like Frank. "For Tony?"

Donna leaned her hands on the wide windowsill and looked out. There was a network of buildings across the way, and an expressway running down the middle. Cars were zooming quickly in both directions. Life was whizzing by in both directions. And she was up here, looking down. Safe. Isolated.

She wanted to keep it that way.

She turned back to look at Lisa. "*Because* of Tony."

"I don't understand."

How could she bear to tell Lisa what it had been like? What it had felt like to find Tony's lifeless body that morning? What it felt like knowing that she had been to blame for what had happened?

That was just it. She couldn't.

The day nurse had left Lisa's chart up on the board for the three-to-eleven shift. Donna looked at it without seeing any of the notations. She shrugged helplessly. "I can't go through being left again."

Lisa tried a different approach. "I guess you could ask him to be immortal for you, but I don't think either one of you will meet with a whole lot of success there." She pressed the hand control and the upper portion of the mattress rose, propping her up. "Honey, everyone dies. All we can hope for is that life is enjoyable while we're here."

This wasn't getting them anywhere and Donna saw that Lisa was tired out. "Stop philosophizing and just get well." She bent over and kissed her sister-in-law's cheek. "I'll see you tomorrow."

"Coward," Lisa chided softly.

"Yes," Donna said honestly. "I am."

Lisa sighed, dropping the subject for now. "Bring me some chocolate when you come back. All they let me have here are liquids."

Donna eyed the intravenous bottles. Frank had told her that Lisa had developed peritonitis, as well. One bottle was for antibiotics, the other for nourishment. "When you're ready."

Lisa did her best to look sorrowful. "I'm ready, I'm ready."

Donna laughed as she crossed to the door. She hoped that Frank and the boys weren't too far away. "See you tomorrow." She paused at the open door. "I'm glad you're all right."

Lisa nodded. "Yeah, me, too."

Chapter Ten

To Frank's surprise, Greg finally returned. Frank had been trying the man's telephone number out of habit every other day. When he'd finally received a human response rather than the annoying answering machine, Frank had been quick to make plans for a get-together.

Eager to make up for the unavoidable delay, Greg took the day off. The two spent the time reminiscing and going over old times. There had been a great many of them. Throughout it all, Frank found himself missing Donna.

As the evening wore on, Frank discovered that he and Greg really had grown apart and gone their separate ways in the past five years. Though they were friendly, they were no longer friends in the deep sense of the word. That part was gone. Both admitted, after a second evening out, that all they had in common now was the past.

Frank was more interested in the present. And the future. A future with Donna.

"I wish you luck with her," Greg had said in parting. "Better than mine's been. Two and zero. But that doesn't stop me from looking."

Frank knew he didn't have to go on looking. He just had to convince Donna.

"Keep me posted," Greg had requested as they parted. Frank fully intended to. After all, if it hadn't been for Greg's letter, none of this would have evolved.

Things just continued to slide away from her, one link hooking up onto another, creating a chain that seemed to stretch endlessly before her. It was a little, Donna thought as she rifled through the paperwork she'd brought home with her yesterday, like being caught up inside a Nintendo game where there was always another drawbridge to cross or one more fireball to escape.

It wasn't the paperwork she was thinking about. It was her feelings for Frank.

She couldn't call an end to this, no matter how hard she tried. Her resolve seemed to *dis*solve each time she was near Frank.

But then again, he would leave on his own accord, she thought. It was only a matter of time. And she was bracing herself against that even as she told herself that she welcomed it, welcomed the tranquillity it would bring. When he left, that would be the end to her inner turmoil. This was only an interlude, and she was determined to keep it that way.

She glanced at Frank, sitting on the sofa, watching cartoons with her youngest. He actually looked as if he were enjoying the show. "Just how long *are* you planning on staying in Seattle?" Frank looked at her. She faltered just a touch. "Don't you have to be getting back?"

It seemed highly improbable to her that Frank could continue postponing his departure without any repercussions, even if he *did* work with his sister. Just how small *was* Wilmington Falls, anyway?

She wanted him to remain here. He could see that in her eyes, taste it on her lips, yet at the same time, she was practically giving him the bum's rush. The lady was slowly sapping his patience.

Cartoon over, he rose and crossed to her desk. "I haven't taken a vacation, other than a scattered day here and there, in years. When I arrived in Seattle, Jeannie told me that she'd taken on the nurse practitioner for a month." His smile was nothing short of smug. "By my calculations, that leaves me a day or two to hang around and help Taylor out with his lessons."

And drive me utterly crazy, she thought in despair. If only her other emotions weren't so strong. If only she were free to care, to love like any other woman.

But she wasn't.

Still, she was like so much kindling when he looked at her. He didn't even have to touch her. His eyes took care of that for him.

Frank smiled as he saw the warmth bloom in her eyes. "You know, it's come to my belated attention that you and I need a night out on the town." He wanted to take her somewhere dark and intimate, where waiters forgot to come over and the night was endless.

"Tonight?" Why was it that every time he came near her, breathing became something she had to actively concentrate on? "The talent show is on tonight."

He knew that better than she did. All morning, Taylor had been vacillating between cockiness and fear as he practiced his numbers. "I meant some other night."

She didn't want to be alone with Frank. She was too vulnerable as it was. "We'll discuss it when the time comes."

He slid the back of his hand along her cheek. "The time may already be here." He said it so softly, she thought it was slipping under her very skin.

"Frank, I need help with the last song you taught me. It's not going right." Taylor's distress call echoed from the family room.

Frank was tempted to steal just a moment more with Donna, but he knew that the moment would blossom into something longer. He didn't have that luxury available to him. Yet.

He inclined his head toward the family room. "Duty calls."

She nodded, wishing her ears would clear up. She kept hearing this rushing sound. It was the echo of her pulse throbbing. She was either coming down with the flu, or something far more dangerous to her health.

"Better answer it."

"Mom, where's my denim jacket?" Taylor wailed from his room. The digital clock on his bureau was flipping minutes by at an incredible rate. His palms were sticky and he'd almost thrown up his dinner, not that he had eaten very much to begin with.

Donna fumbled as she fastened her remaining earring. Getting Stephen ready for the talent show had put her behind schedule. Frank, naturally, had arrived early. She had left him with Lisa in the living room, hoping to keep the man out of her hair until she got dressed. She was as nervous as a cat on a fence looking down at a bulldog.

She dropped her earring on the light gray rug and muttered under her breath as she searched for it.

"Where you left it," she called out her answer impatiently to Taylor.

"Momm!"

The plaintive cry told her that Taylor had absolutely no idea where he had left it. Typical man, she thought affectionately.

She scooped up the earring from the rug and hurried out. "I'm coming."

Threading the post through the tiny hole, she secured the back as she entered Taylor's room. His shirttails were hanging out and his hair was standing up on end. An open jar of mousse lay on the lip of the sink in his bathroom, surrounded by several dabs of foam.

Moving straight to his closet, Donna pushed three hangers aside and retrieved the missing jacket. She handed the hanger to Taylor and he mumbled something that might or might not have been "thanks."

Her heart went out to him. "You'll be great."

He only muttered something unintelligible under his breath.

With a sigh, Donna left her son to his fussing.

When Donna entered the living room, she saw Stephen wiggling as if a worm had suddenly been dropped down his back. He was trying to get comfortable inside his jacket and was failing miserably. Lisa, just barely home from the hospital, was sitting on the sofa, the remote in her hand. She looked prepared to spend the evening with the television set while the rest of the family sat sweating it out in the school auditorium, Donna thought enviously.

Lisa looked at Donna as the latter walked in. "I wish I was going with you."

But that was impossible. The doctor had left strict orders that she was to take it easy the first week at home and she knew that no one was about to let her ignore those orders.

Donna pressed her lips together. "I just wish it was over with." She placed a hand over her stomach, a stomach that churned and turned over each time she thought of her firstborn up there on stage, alone, tonight.

"Nervous, Mama?" Frank asked with an affectionate laugh.

She nodded. "Terrified." Then she blushed, knowing how stupid that had to sound to him. "It's just a little auditorium with a small audience." She wasn't sure who she was trying to convince with that—Frank or herself.

"Yes, but it's your son there." Frank squeezed Donna's hand, his eyes warm and crinkling. "He'll be fine."

The fact that he could understand what she was going through instead of laughing her reaction off as being silly comforted her immensely.

"You really think so?" She wanted so badly for Taylor to be good tonight. It meant so much to him and he had practiced so hard these past few weeks.

She already knew that, he thought. "You heard him play."

"Yes, but that was for you," she reminded him. For a moment, she was completely honest, with no walls—no barriers—between them. "I think for you, he'd do anything."

Frank shrugged it off, but she could see that her words touched him. "He certainly practiced enough to get this right and he's got a talent for it."

Stephen was still moving around as though someone was raising an ant farm along his shoulder blades. He planted himself in front of his mother.

"How come I have to wear this?" The question bordered on belligerent as he tugged on his tie.

She straightened the tie he had twisted to the side and centered it. "We're all dressing up, honey."

Donna slanted a look toward Frank. They certainly were, she thought. She'd never seen him in a jacket and tie before and she had to admit that the man very nearly stole her breath away. He was even more handsome dressed up than when he was slumming.

Was she crazy, she wondered, trying to resist this feeling that kept coming over her with the relentlessness of an avalanche? Any other woman would probably kill to have this man in her life, however temporarily.

But she wasn't any other woman. She was her, Donna McCullough, and she knew her own limitations.

And her own nightmares.

"Taylor isn't dressed up," Stephen protested. He pulled away, but left his tie where it was, even though he felt it was choking him.

She thought of the denim jacket she had unearthed. "He is for Taylor." She raised her voice. "Taylor, we'd better hurry up if we want to make it to the auditorium on time."

There was no response. A minute later, Taylor came out, nervously clutching the guitar in his hand. He wasn't wearing his jacket and his shirt was still half unbuttoned.

"See? He's not dressed up!" Stephen cried, vindicated as he pointed to his brother.

Taylor's face was pale as vanilla frosting. "I'm not going."

"What?" The question rose to Donna's lips without her even being conscious of forming it.

Taylor swallowed back tears in his throat. He could taste them. "It was a dumb idea in the first place. I'm not going.'' The guitar dropped from his sweaty hand. He stared at it accusingly, then turned and ran.

Donna and Lisa exchanged looks. ''Now what?'' Donna breathed.

''Stage fright.'' Frank crossed to the guitar and picked it up.

If Taylor was this afraid, then they'd just forget about it. She didn't want to put her son through this kind of misery. ''Maybe we'd better not push this.'' She didn't realize that she was unconsciously including Frank in her decision by saying ''we.''

But he shook his head slowly, taking it upon himself to overrule her. ''There's a time to run and a time to stop.'' He looked at Donna very significantly. ''If Taylor runs from this, he won't be able to distinguish between the two when he gets older.''

Frank left the room, leaving her breathless. Donna could have sworn, just for an instant, that he was talking to her *about* her, not about Taylor.

Frank knocked lightly on the doorjamb since the door was open, and then entered the small bedroom. Taylor sat on his desk, his head propped up on fisted hands, elbows on his knees. He looked absolutely miserable.

''Hey, Taylor.''

''Hey, yourself,'' Taylor mumbled. He raised only his eyes to Frank's face. ''You disappointed in me?'' He fully expected the man to say yes.

''No.'' There was no hesitation in Frank's voice. ''Just disappointed that all that hard work you put in in the last two weeks is going to be wasted.'' He put the guitar down and picked up an orange Nerf ball, casually tossing it through the small hoop that was mounted on the back of the closet door. ''And maybe I'm a little disappointed that no one else will get the chance to see how good you've become.'' He bent to retrieve the ball, then tossed it in again, this time from the far side of the room.

''I'm not that good.''

Frank picked up the foam ball and offered it to Taylor. "I think you are."

Taylor frowned. He measured, then tossed. The ball tottered on the red plastic rim before sinking in. "You have to say that."

"No, I don't."

The low, quiet tone had Taylor looking up at Frank. Fears came tumbling out. "What if I mess up?"

"You won't." Frank's voice was firm, confident. "If you hit a wrong chord, you keep going. Nobody else in the audience will notice, anyway." He threw the ball aside and turned to face Taylor. "What they *will* notice is if you stop. Or don't show up."

Frank placed his hands on Taylor's shoulders and looked at him squarely. "Taylor, everyone's afraid when they go in front of a crowd."

Taylor didn't believe that. "Not you."

Frank laughed and shook his head, remembering his first time. And his second. Trying to brazen it out, he'd still been a distinct shade of green. "Oh, yes, me. Most definitely me."

Taylor's eyes grew round and his mouth gaped open. "You're kidding."

"Taylor, listen to me." Frank inclined his head closer to the boy, his eyes intent. "Nerves are a good thing. They keep you sharp, on your toes. The greatest performers in the world have stage fright. Some all the time, some once in a while, but nobody, *nobody* is immune to it."

"I don't like stage fright. It's icky." Taylor put his hand over his stomach. He felt like throwing up. "Why do they do it?"

One of the mysteries of life, Frank thought, amused. "Because they love performing more than not performing," he said simply. That was the reason in his case. "They love it more than feeling comfortable."

He hooked an arm affectionately around the boy's neck and drew him gently from his perch. "It's just something in their blood, something they have to do." He looked into the innocent face and saw just a touch of himself, years removed. "Not everyone has a calling, Taylor. Some people float through life without any direction. Wanting to perform is a direction. *Wanting* to do anything is a direction. Don't just give up because it's difficult or frightening. You'll only have regrets if you don't try, and you won't be very proud of yourself for dropping out."

Taylor licked his lips as he eyed the guitar. "Think I should go tonight?"

He wanted to shout yes. But it had to be Taylor's call. "What do you think?"

Taylor raised his eyes, his brows disappearing beneath the fringe of his hair and suddenly, he looked very, very young and unsure of himself. "I think I should."

Frank laughed, relieved. He helped him on with his jacket. "That makes two of us. Now let's go and knock their socks off."

Taylor knew Frank had said he would, but he needed to hear it again. "You'll be there?"

"Sure I'll be there. I'll be the guy clapping his hands off."

Taylor began to feel better. Some of his bravado started to return. "Even if I make a mistake?"

There was no question about it. "Even if you make a mistake."

Taylor walked into the living room ahead of Frank and looked sheepishly at his mother. Donna didn't know what to say, what she *could* say to follow Frank's act. She knew it had to have been good, to have the boy here and ready to go. Falling back on instincts, she just put her arms around her son and hugged him.

For a moment, because he was young and needed it, Taylor let her. But then he stepped back, remembering that he was eleven and mature. "Mom, you're messing up my jacket."

She gave him an affectionate smile. "Sorry. I forgot myself."

Frank, who had followed with the guitar, handed it to Taylor. "Let's get this show on the road."

* * *

They left Taylor at the rear entrance of the school auditorium, where he was immediately swallowed up by the crowd of milling children, two teachers and one teacher's aide.

In the auditorium, Frank led them to three seats in the third row, just off center. An usherette in white anklets, Mary Janes and a pale pink party dress handed them each a dark blue program as they took their seats.

Donna skimmed the list. Taylor's name appeared eighth on the program. Great. There was just enough time for Donna's stomach to tie itself into a knot three times over.

As each performer left the darkened stage, she could hear her heart drumming in her ears, pounding through all of her. They were that much closer to Taylor's number.

Finally it was his turn.

Taylor walked out onto the stage that had been preset with a single stool. A microphone stood before it and nothing but a long, green curtain was behind it. Donna's heart tightened in her chest.

She leaned over to Frank. "He looks so small up there."

He liked the feel of her leaning toward him, of her whispering tiny confidentialities in his ear. "It's relative."

She turned to him slightly and almost brushed her lips against his cheek. She drew back. "Because the stage is large?"

He smiled. "No, because you're his relative and it colors your vision."

"Shh, he's starting." She hushed him nervously. Crossing her fingers, she turned forward.

Taylor tapped the microphone and the thud vibrated across the auditorium. She saw him take a deep breath, as if bracing himself for the plunge.

"For my first number," Taylor addressed the audience, his voice sounding thinner, reedier than usual, "I'd like to play 'Greensleeves'. For my mom." He looked out at the audience and imagined her there. The glare of the lights blotted out even the closest faces.

A few titters were heard coupled with "aws" in response to Taylor's dedication. Donna blinked back tears and sniffed.

"He hasn't started yet," Frank whispered to her.

"Yes, he has," she murmured in reply, her heart brimming. Without realizing it, she threaded her hand through Frank's.

Donna felt every nervous twinge that passed through her son at that moment. She squeezed Frank's hand as the first chords of the ballad were strummed. Her grip remained tight throughout the entire set. Three numbers, each one better than the last. Taylor had begun haltingly, but as he lost himself in the music, his fingering became more confident. There were no mistakes in the last number.

When he finished, the applause from the audience was genuine rather than just polite and empathetic as it had been for several of the other performers.

Donna clapped until her hands felt numb. Stephen was standing up, cheering beside her.

"Look at him," she said to Frank, her eyes on Taylor. "He looks so proud."

Frank's hearty applause blended with hers. "He has a right to be." He dropped his hands to his side and flexed the left one.

Donna looked down at his hand, surprised that he'd stopped applauding. "What's the matter?"

He laughed as the applause died away. They watched Taylor leave the stage. Two girls in matching costumes came out as a teacher set up a tape deck in front of the stage.

"You've got a better grip than Rosemary had in the middle of a contraction." He turned toward her as the lights dimmed again. "At one point I thought you were going to break my hand off altogether."

She smiled ruefully, inclining her head so that only he could hear her. "I was just nervous for him."

"I could tell."

Donna could hear the laughter in his voice.

* * *

She could hardly wait for the entire program to be over. When it was, she, Frank and Stephen made their way through the maze of parents, siblings and various assorted relatives and friends milling around backstage to collect Taylor. They found him talking to a group of older boys who Donna assumed had been the bullies he had wanted to show up two weeks ago. Everyone appeared to be the best of friends now.

Mission accomplished, she mused.

Taylor saw them and quickly said goodbye to his friends. He was three inches off the ground as he hurried over to his family.

"Did ya hear?" Taylor crowed, eager for their approval. "Did ya?"

Donna hugged him, then carefully let go in case that embarrassed him in front of his newly won friends. "We sure did."

There wasn't a trace of embarrassment evident. Only pride. "I was great."

Frank laughed, clamping a hand on his shoulder. "That you were."

Stephen was hopping from foot to foot, desperate to be a part of this winner's circle. "Can I hold the guitar, Tay? Can I?"

Taylor turned toward him and benevolently handed over the instrument. "Sure, Stephen. Just don't hurt it."

Donna couldn't ever remember Taylor calling his brother by his formal name.

Rather than give any answer, Stephen took the guitar reverently into his hands and then struggled to hold it upright. Frank gently threaded his fingers through the case's handle and subtly lifted it with the boy.

"Did you like it, Mom?" Taylor asked as they made their way outside.

"Yes, very much." The dark night air felt sweet as it enveloped them in its velvety glove. A breeze was stirring to sweep the mustiness of the day away.

"Which part?" Taylor asked eagerly, turning to face her as he walked backward to the car.

She laid a hand on his shoulder to keep him from walking into people. "All of it."

He was fairly beaming. "I dedicated the first one to you."

She blinked back tears again. One escaped anyway, trickling down her cheek. "Yes, I know." She wiped it away with her hand.

Taylor couldn't understand why his mother cried when she was happy. Tears were only if you got hurt, and then only if no one was looking. "Aw, Mom, you're not supposed to cry."

She took in a deep breath, then smiled at him. He was getting so big, she thought. He wasn't her baby anymore. "Sorry, occupational hazard. I loved the song." She brushed her lips against his cheek. "Thank you." From now on, "Greensleeves" would belong to *them*—to her and Taylor. Life went on.

When they reached the car, Taylor abruptly stopped his exuberant narrative about what went on backstage before and after his number and turned toward Frank. Unabashed, he flung himself into Frank's arms. "Thanks."

Surprised, Frank allowed himself a moment to absorb the warmth. He patted Taylor on the back. "Don't mention it. Besides, I didn't do anything. You were the one playing."

Taylor wasn't so full of tonight and the applause that he didn't remember how it all had come about. "You taught me. And you made me go."

"No." Frank shook his head. "*You* made you go. I couldn't make you do anything you didn't want to do." He slid a finger down the boy's nose. "Remember that."

As Taylor hugged him again, Frank looked over Taylor's head at Donna and wondered if she understood what he was saying.

Chapter Eleven

Frank walked into his hotel room, tired after a grueling game of tennis. Greg had called him out of the blue yesterday to offer him his club key. Frank could be his guest while he remained in Seattle. Delighted, Frank had coaxed Donna into coming with him. Donna had managed to reschedule her day to allow for an hour in the late afternoon, and had met him at the athletic club near the airport. A very exhausting hour.

It was wonderful, he thought as he flopped down on the bed, snaring a little time alone with her, even if he *had* been chasing a ball most of the time. He felt drained. It had been a long time since he had played tennis. Her form had been far better than this.

Her form, he thought with a slow, lazy smile, was excellent.

Frank laced his fingers beneath his head, cradling it. He was breaking down her barriers. It wasn't easy, but she was more relaxed with him now. And she laughed. As long as he didn't mention anything permanent.

That was going to have to change.

Frank knew he had stretched as far as he could, played out the line as far as it would go. The whimsical vacation he had taken for a week was now inching up on its fourth. He couldn't expect Jeannie to wait forever for him to return.

A distant, but persistent gnawing guilt had Frank reaching for the small, Princess telephone on the nightstand and tapping out the numbers to Jeannie's home.

The telephone barely rang once.

"'Lo?"

Frank smiled to himself as Mollie's very authoritative, very young voice filled the receiver. "Hi, Mollie. It's Uncle Frank. Is Mommy around?"

"Hi, Uncle Frank!" Her pleasure fairly spilled out over the connection.

In his mind's eye he could see her, propping the telephone between her shoulder and ear, holding on to the mouthpiece the way she did when she was attempting to imitate her mother.

"No, Mommy's still at the clinic. Working." The precocious young lady faded as the little girl emerged. "When are you coming home, Uncle Frank? I miss you and since you've been gone, Mommy's never home anymore, either." She paused, as if wondering if she should betray a secret. "Daddy tries hard, but he makes pretty awful dinners for us."

It struck Frank as incredible how easily children seemed to flow with things. How easily Mollie had taken to calling Shane Daddy, almost from the first. He wondered what it would take to have Taylor and Stephen call him Dad?

If the reason ever arose.

Guilt took another chunk out of him as he thought over the meaning of Mollie's words. "Mommy's pretty busy these days, huh?"

Mollie sighed dramatically, and he could have sworn she sounded like an old woman.

"All the time. The first nurse left and the next one, Mommy said—" Mollie strove to get the words just right "—didn't work out. Then there was another one. But she left after a day. Now Mommy doesn't stop long enough to have lunch with me anymore. Grandma says she's getting too thin.''

Each time he'd called Jeannie at the clinic, she had assured him that everything was running smoothly. She had actually encouraged him to stay here in Seattle, saying she could handle whatever came up. Why had she lied? Why hadn't she said anything about how hectic things were?

The guilt mushroomed like bread baking in the oven with too much yeast added to it. It was time to stop indulging himself.

He made his decision.

''Tell Mommy for me that I'm coming home.'' He rose to his feet. Uncertainties nipped at the plans forming in his head. ''I'll be there tomorrow evening by the latest. Goodbye, honey.'' He was about to hang up when he heard a voice in the background at the other end.

''Wait, Uncle Frank, don't hang up. Daddy wants to talk to you.'' There was the sound of shuffling as the receiver changed hands.

Cradling the phone against his own neck and shoulder, Frank took his suitcase out of the closet and tossed it on the bed. His brother-in-law came on the line as he unzipped the cloth bag. ''Shane? Are you there?''

''Hi, stranger. How's it going? Hold it,'' Shane said, stopping Frank before anything could be said. ''Mollie, wash your hands. Dinner's almost ready. Sorry, I'm back,'' he apologized to Frank.

Frank wondered if the small groan in the background was his imagination, or if it was Mollie's reaction to dinner.

''The question is,'' Frank said, getting back to Shane's greeting, ''how's Jeannie? Mollie's just been filling me in. She says that the nurses are dropping like flies at the clinic.''

From the slight pause at the other end, it was obvious that Shane felt uncomfortable about being caught in the middle. Loyalty to his wife warred with the truth. Truth won.

''Yeah, well, the count is three and zero. She doesn't have one at the moment, but you know Jeannie. Stubborn to the end.''

Yes, and liable to work herself to a frazzle. "But why—?" Frank began.

Shane laughed. How had Jeannie put it? "She wanted you to have a chance to pursue your angel. Ever since we met, she's been a great believer in going with instincts and destiny. She had this hunch that maybe Donna was yours."

Too bad Donna didn't seem to quite see it that way, Frank thought. But whether she did or not, he had obligations to fulfill. "Well, if she's my destiny, then it'll find a way to work itself out. Tell Jeannie I'm coming home tomorrow."

"That's great!" The relief ebbed out of Shane's voice, coaxed away by concern. "You don't sound too good. Is everything all right?"

"That remains to be seen." Suddenly Frank felt like a sheriff, strapping on his gun and facing high noon. "I'll see you tomorrow night."

"Be sure you call when you land. I'll pick you up at the airport," Shane promised.

The airport was in Riverdale. "That's a twenty-mile trip, you don't—"

Shane cut him short. "Hey, I'm from L.A. remember? I can do twenty miles in my sleep. See you tomorrow, brother-in-law."

"Yeah, right."

Frank hung up and then sighed as he stared at the interior of his suitcase.

He wasn't about to let his sister continue working herself to death just because he was chasing rainbows. He was a grown man with responsibilities. Responsibilities he had let slide far too long.

He was going to have to tell Donna that he was leaving. And hope that she'd finally agree to a future together.

When he arrived at Donna's house, dinner was just being served. Stephen ushered him into the kitchen, talking even faster than usual. Frank crossed to the place where he normally sat and ran his hands along the back of the chair, a knot forming in his stomach.

He didn't want to ask and hear Donna say no.

Donna turned just in time to see Frank enter. Between her oven-mittened hands, she held a casserole dish filled to the brim with chicken tetrazzini.

"Hey, why the long face? It's not my tuna casserole," she teased as she eased the dish onto the table. She was obviously pleased to see him. "After that rousing game this afternoon, I thought you deserved a treat. I beat him six love," she crowed to the others.

Her eyes sparkled. He'd made a difference in her life, she thought. He'd made her laugh again, and forget, for a little while, all the things that haunted her.

Maybe he'd tell them after dinner, Frank decided. No use in spoiling the meal. Besides, he wanted to talk to Donna alone. Now wasn't the time, with everyone around the kitchen table.

Lisa tapped the side of her glass with a spoon, cutting through the various threads of conversation at the table just as Donna sat down. "I have an announcement to make. I dropped eight pounds." She grinned as she spooned out her portion of the casserole. "And you all know what that means."

Together they chimed, "More chocolate."

"You'd get along beautifully with my niece," Frank said after the laughter died down. He helped himself to a minuscule portion. The meal smelled wonderful, but his appetite was nonexistent. "Mollie loves chocolate."

Stephen was attempting to wrap a long strand of spaghetti around his fork and losing. "Yeah?" He cocked his head, sucking the strand in the hard way. "How old is she?"

"Mollie's six." Going on twenty-eight, Frank added silently.

Donna handed Stephen his napkin. There was sauce on his chin. Vigorous wiping in an isolated spot only managed to get half off his face. His attention was divided between the meal and Frank's niece. Neither of which necessitated cleanliness. "When was she six?"

Frank had to stop for a minute before he remembered. "May second."

Victory split his face into a grin as male dominance triumphed. "Ha, I'm older. I was born in April." He wound his fork into another strand, faring just as poorly. Stephen looked up at Frank hopefully. "Can I meet Mollie sometime?"

"I don't know." Frank looked toward Donna and saw that she was studying him thoughtfully. "That depends."

"On what?" Taylor raised his brows, his interest piqued.

"On your mother." Frank saw that Donna had lowered her eyes and was suddenly intent on eating her dinner. He turned his attention toward the children. "You could take a trip to Wilmington Falls."

Stephen rolled that over in his head. "Can't Mollie come out here?"

Jeannie would only travel to Seattle if he remained, and he had already made up his mind that he wouldn't. Couldn't. Wilmington Falls was more his speed now, where everyone knew everyone else and the lure of the "big city" could be satisfied when the whim moved, by driving to the next town, not by looking out of a window.

"I suppose so," Frank conceded as he finished the small amount on his plate. "But her mother's a doctor in the clinic there. The same place where I'm a nurse," he added, and saw Stephen stifle a giggle behind his hand. Stephen still thought that a man being a nurse was pretty funny. "Things get a little hectic when she leaves for too long." He felt another shaft of guilt. He might as well have been talking about himself, he thought.

"Oh." Stephen took the information in stride. "I guess we'll have to go there, then." He turned to look at his mother. "Can we, Mom? Please?"

Frank had done it again. He'd put her on the spot. He was making her sound like the heavy, she thought, slanting Frank a look. She shrugged vaguely. "Maybe. Someday."

The evasive tone told Frank a great deal. More than he wanted to know.

* * *

"Hey, Frank, Mom rented a new video for us to watch. It's got that big guy with all those muscles in it," Taylor told Frank excitedly as he left the table.

"You know," Lisa prompted, amused. "The one whose last name is almost as broad as his shoulders."

"Sounds good." Frank tried to put enthusiasm into his voice. "But maybe later, okay? I want to help your mother with the dishes."

Stephen was already sliding out of his chair with a fluid motion that said bones were only optional at his age. "Okay. C'mon, Tay, I'll show you how to freeze-frame."

"I already know how to freeze-frame, Step-On." Taylor hurried after him.

Lisa looked over her shoulder as she followed the boys out of the kitchen. "Play nice." Her words were aimed at Donna and Frank, not Taylor and Stephen.

For a moment, silence simmered in the kitchen, a direct contrast to the activity in the next room. Donna gathered several plates together and brought them to the sink to rinse off. She felt the tension rising in her shoulders. The light-hearted feeling she'd had these past few days was gone now. She'd clung to it, to the laughter Frank created in her life, because she had known it was just temporary and required no commitment from her. It was safe and felt wonderful.

But now it was over.

She'd known this was coming. Had counted on it coming. But now that it was here, there was this emptiness suddenly growing inside her, threatening to swallow her up.

Donna kept her back to Frank as she worked. "You're leaving, aren't you?"

Her tone was low, flat. Frank couldn't tell how she felt.

"Yes."

The last dish had been rinsed. She watched the stream of water cascade over her fingers as if the sight were fascinating. As if chaos weren't rioting within her.

"When?"

"Tomorrow morning. I called Jeannie just after I'd gotten in from the game." He leaned around her and closed the tap.

Donna raised her eyes to him, her heart in her throat. "And?"

"I didn't get her."

Donna turned around to face him. His eyes searched her face for a sign that his leaving made any sort of a difference to her. Or had he just been investing all his time for nothing? No, she cared. He knew she did. But there was still this barrier between them, this wall he couldn't breach. He tried, anyway. He had to. Time was running out.

"She was still at the clinic. She'd been at the clinic every night. I spoke to Mollie and found out that Jeannie's been working longer hours than usual and that the nurses the agency's been sending haven't been working out. Shane said Jeannie didn't even have one right now."

Donna brushed past him and reached for the dish towel. She slowly dried her hands as if that were the only thing on her mind. As if there weren't a war raging inside her. She blew out a long breath. "I guess, then, you'd better go home."

He couldn't believe she was actually saying that. There was no feeling in her voice. No remorse. Nothing. "Just like that?"

She swallowed, wishing her mouth didn't feel so dry. Wishing her throat wasn't so full of tears. She forced a smile to her lips as she looked up at him. "No, it would help if you were on a plane."

Damn it, why was she being like this? "This isn't a time for joking."

She threw the towel aside, angry to feel this way, angry at being trapped in two worlds, wanting him, afraid of wanting him. Fear of attachment, of the ultimate pain that brought, had a very real, very hard grip on her and she couldn't break free.

Not even for him.

"What do you want me to say? 'Stay Frank. Stay with me and the boys'?" She shook her head. "I can't do that. This isn't your world." To ask him to remain wouldn't be fair to either one of them. She didn't know if she was even capable of giving him what he wanted. She didn't know if she could *ever* break free of the chains that bound her.

He took her into his arms, hoping that physical contact could somehow melt this force field she retained around her heart. She loved him; he *knew* she loved him. She hadn't said as much, but he didn't have that good an imagination to have conjured up the responses he'd felt from her in the past few weeks.

"You could come with me. Just for a little while, you and the boys," he coaxed, running his hand through her hair. "You could see what it was like. Maybe decide to stay."

He was making this too hard. She shook her head. "I can't do that, either."

He was fighting for his life here and he knew it. Pride told him to back away, but something else was goading him to extend himself further than he would ever have thought possible. "We're not as backward there as you might think."

She pulled away. "I know. You've already told me all about it." She shut her eyes for a moment, squeezing back the tears. When she opened them again, her eyes shone with them. "It's not a matter of place, Frank, it's a matter of me."

He struggled with his temper. Why was she denying something they both knew was right? Bitter humor curved his mouth.

"You're the one I'd like to go with me. You're not even giving this a chance." Because he wanted to shake her, shake her until the sense returned to her head, he shoved his hands into his pockets. "The boys can adjust. Wilmington Falls is great for kids, and it's growing." He saw that his words just weren't penetrating. "Not so fast that it takes your breath away, but we keep the livestock in the barn now. They only eat at the table with us on Sundays."

She saw the hurt, the anger growing in his eyes and knew she had put it there. Guilt warred with her sense of self-preservation. Her mind searched frantically for a plausible excuse. *Any* excuse.

"I'm not implying that you're hayseeds. But I just can't pull up stakes like this. There's the boys' school..." Her voice trailed off, hollow.

None of it held any water. "The school year's almost over."

"What about my charter service?" she challenged suddenly. She'd worked so hard to put that together again. And it had saved her. Working there had kept her sane after Tony had died.

"You could relocate. I don't know." He threw up his hands. "Damn it, things could be arranged. If you wanted them to be. If you cared about us."

She shook her head and then took a deep breath. It didn't help. The pain in her heart wouldn't leave. "There can't be an 'us.'"

"Why? Why can't there be an 'us'?" If she gave him an answer he could understand, that he could deal with, he'd leave her alone. He'd turn and walk away, no matter what it cost him.

But he knew that she couldn't give him a good reason. Under the fear in her eyes, he saw that she wanted this as much as he did. How could he make *her* see that? What words could he use to break through to her?

Patiently, he began again. "I'm thirty-two years old, Donna, and I've never asked a woman to marry me. This is no longer a society where you're incomplete if you don't have a wife and 2.3 kids. I have enough in my life to feel that it's full. Or I did." He sifted her hair through his fingers as he looked into her eyes. "I'm asking you to—"

Panic welled within her. Donna pressed her fingers to his lips, silencing him. "No, don't."

He pushed her hand away. Anger flashed in his eyes. "Don't what? Don't ask you to marry me? Don't love you? What?"

Donna pressed her lips together, holding back a sob. "I don't want to love you, Frank."

"I didn't know that it was something you could turn on and off like a spigot. I thought it either happened or didn't happen." He saw the misery in her eyes and felt guilty for having put it there, but couldn't stop himself. He was angry with her, angry that she was denying them something that could be wonderful. "I certainly wasn't looking to fall in love, but I did and it was with you." And now there was hell to pay, he thought. "Call it fate, serendipity, Cupid's touch or voodoo, but I fell for you from the very first moment I saw you. I just didn't know how hard or for how long. That's what I had to explore." He looked at her solemnly. He was never going to love anyone the way he did her. "And now I've found out."

She didn't want to hurt him. She didn't want to hurt anyone. "It's just infatuation."

He knew what she was doing and he wasn't about to let her shrug it away so easily. "Infatuation's a wonderful thing, but I passed that three weeks ago. I *love* you, Donna, warts and all."

"Warts?"

The smile that crept along his lips didn't begin to reach his eyes. "You're not exactly the most easygoing person. And you keep running from common sense."

She needed something to do, something to keep her hands occupied. Methodically, she began stacking the dishes in the dishwasher, but she hardly registered what she was doing. "No, this makes perfect sense. If you get burned, you don't play with matches again."

How could she say that? Didn't she know what she'd been doing these past few weeks? "But you played, Donna, you played." No amount of denial could change that for either of them.

"Yes, I did," she said quietly. "Once. And I thought I had come up with the perfect life. I had two beautiful children, a good business going and a husband I adored at my side." Inwardly she braced herself before continuing. It was time to tell him the truth. To let him know just who he had fallen in love with.

She turned to look at him, and there were fresh tears in her eyes. "Do you know how my husband died, Frank?"

Her voice was oddly empty. Apprehension filled him. "No."

"I killed him."

Frank could only stare at her. "You?" That couldn't be true. There had to be some explanation.

"Yes." Looking away from him, she hesitated. But she had come too far to back off now. "Tony took over the business when my father died. He had these big dreams, a fleet of planes with our emblem on them." A sad smile played on her lips and faded. "And he overextended us." As she spoke, it all came rushing back to her. She had to struggle to keep from crying.

"Every time I questioned him about it, he became defensive, telling me not to worry, that everything was going to be fine." She pressed her lips together to hold back the tears in her soul. "We were mortgaged up to the hilt and the bank was threatening to foreclose. We had a huge argument when the notice came in the mail. He stormed out and left the house. I didn't try to stop him. Tony didn't come home all night." She turned her gaze back to Frank. "It took me that long to cool off, so I didn't try to look for him. And I should have. Oh, I should have."

She closed her eyes, but that only made things worse. She saw Tony then. Clearly. Donna shuddered and opened her eyes.

"I came into the office early the next morning and...he...was...there. He was just...hanging there." Donna covered her mouth to keep the sob back. When Frank stepped forward to hold her, she shook her head violently. She had to say this, to finally get it out. If he held her now, she would crumble.

"He left a note, saying that I was right, he had made a mess of everything. He was too ashamed to face me." She swallowed the tears. "And this way, he didn't have to, ever again." Her voice hitched. "I drove him to that. Don't you see? I can't just start over again. I killed him."

Frank remained where he was, feeling helpless, aching to make her understand how wrong she was. "Donna, you had nothing to do with his weakness. That was *his* doing, not yours. Another man would have tried to find a way out."

She grew defensive of her husband's memory. "Tony was a good man."

He was bordering on desperation. "I'm not saying that he wasn't. I'm just saying that I am, too. And I deserve a chance, Donna. We both do."

"I can't risk it." She shook her head. "I can't risk loving anyone again. And I don't even deserve to. Just go." She turned away and continued placing dishes, one behind the other, on the rack.

Frank spun her around so hard, the breath whooshed out of her lungs. And then he kissed her. Long and hard and angrily. He let the hunger and despair he felt travel through him to her as he held her close, plundering, taking, trying to hate her.

But he couldn't hate her.

He kissed her, mourning all the moments they wouldn't have, the children they wouldn't beget, the life they wouldn't share.

Then, with an oath, he thrust her from him and tried not to be affected by the small, strangled cry she uttered.

"I have to say goodbye to the boys."

He strode out of the room without looking back.

Frank tried not to think of the expressions on their faces, but they followed him all through the trip home. They crept into his mind at odd moments even after that. Two weeks had gone by and still he couldn't get back to normal, couldn't shake the pall that had fallen over him. Couldn't escape the memory of Taylor's and Stephen's saddened faces.

"I thought you were going to stay here and be our dad," Stephen had said when Frank had gathered him and Taylor to him in the family room to tell them he was leaving.

"Yeah," Taylor echoed. Frank knew that the boy couldn't say anything further because his voice broke in the middle of the one word.

Frank stroked Stephen's hair. Hair so like Donna's. It was harder leaving them than he'd thought. "I've got to get back to work, guys." He tried to keep his voice light. "I've already stayed longer than I should have." *A lot longer.*

Sitting in his lap, Stephen twined his arms around Frank's neck and held on tightly. "Don't go, Frank. You don't have to go back to work. We'll pay you to stay here."

Frank struggled not to give in to the choke hold his emotions had on him. He could feel his heart aching. "It's not the money, Stephen— I've got responsibilities."

But Stephen didn't understand. He only knew that Frank was leaving them. "Can't you get rid of them?"

Frank sighed heavily. Even if he could, it wasn't that simple. Donna had turned her back on him, on them. "No. Some responsibilities you can't get rid of."

Sliding Stephen gently from his lap, he rose. Donna, he knew, was in her room. He had heard the door slam. "I want you boys to be good to your mother and take care of her and your aunt Lisa. Okay?"

They nodded and said nothing further. Kneeling, Frank spread his arms wide and they flung themselves in. For a moment, they held on tightly. Then, slowly, Frank eased away. "Don't forget to keep practicing. Both of you. I expect you to be reading books soon, Stephen. Big ones."

"Will you be back?" Taylor asked suddenly. Hopefully.

"Sure I will," Frank lied.

Lisa cornered him at the door. She laid a hand on his arm. "I'll work on her."

Frank shook his head and smiled sadly at the woman he'd come to look upon as a friend. "No. Thanks for the offer, but this is something she has to come around about by herself. It wouldn't be any good between us if someone has to convince her. I'm not a white elephant at a raffle that you've got to talk her into caring about."

Lisa touched his cheek. Donna was throwing away a good man, she thought. The idiot. "You're sure not that, Handsome." She bit her lip and looked toward the rear of the house. "Donna's still hurting."

He knew that, but there was a time to bury old pain and move on. They *both* knew that. "The pain doesn't get any easier if you don't bury it."

Lisa nodded. "I'll tell her you said that. Anything else you want me to tell her?"

He opened the door. "Yeah. That she's got my number."

And she had, he thought now as he spread a fresh sheet of paper over the examining table. He crumbled up the last sheet, wrinkled with Mrs. Abernathy's imprint. Donna had his number through and through. She just didn't know it. Or if she did, she didn't want to use it.

"Any coffee left, Frank?"

Frank turned to see Jeannie walking into the room. "Just some I was planning on using to repave the driveway with this weekend."

She'd been watching him for a few moments before she entered. Her heart ached for him. Jeannie couldn't remember Frank *ever* being so sad. It was as if another person had returned from Seattle. One who bore little resemblance to the happy-go-lucky brother she had grown up with.

"Sounds like heaven." She nodded toward the small alcove where they kept the coffeemaker. "Join me?"

He sighed as he tossed aside the paper into the wastepaper basket. "Sure, why not?" He followed her into the tiny hall. The alcove was right next to it. All the rooms of the clinic were grouped together like children, huddling with a secret. "I love drinking tar."

She poured him a cup, then one for herself. It looked as if there were sludge on the bottom of the glass pot, but they both liked their coffee strong. Jeannie curved her hands around the white mug, her eyes on his as she brought the coffee to her lips.

"That was the last patient for the day. Mom's already gone home. I've got a little time. Want to talk?"

No, he didn't want to talk. He didn't know what he wanted. Two weeks and he couldn't find a niche for himself in his own home.

He drained his mug without tasting anything. "No. Why don't you go home and I'll clean up around here?"

"It *is* clean, Frank."

Jeannie set the mug down. "She really got to you, didn't she?" He hadn't spoken a word about the woman he'd left behind since he'd returned. Jeannie knew it made the matter that much more serious. She and Frank had *always* talked. About everything.

He sighed and walked over to the window. Two crows were patrolling the wide front lawn like sentries. "Yeah, she did."

Jeannie put her hands into the wide pockets of her lab coat. "So what are you doing here?"

He shrugged, still watching the birds. "You need me."

She came up behind him and placed her hand on his shoulder. "Don't put it on my shoulders, Frank. You're great, but eventually I'll find someone to take your place." Her mouth curved slightly. "Long and hard though the quest might be."

"Thanks." He grinned and Jeannie relaxed a little. Except for Mollie's benefit, he hadn't really smiled since he had returned.

"Relocating isn't the solution," he told her. "Donna doesn't want a permanent relationship. She made it very clear."

Jeannie considered his words for a moment. "Professionally speaking, Frank, I have it on the best authority that if you marry a stupid person, there's a fifty-fifty chance you'll have stupid children." She smiled up at him, love brimming in her eyes. She wished she could make this right for him. But she couldn't. She could only be there for him. "And she's got to be stupid to be turning you down."

He tousled her hair the way he had when they were young. "Thanks, Squirt." He sighed. Life went on, no matter how he felt about it. "Don't worry about me. Things always have a way of working out for the best."

"That was one of Dad's axioms," she recalled fondly.

"Dad was right." He glanced at his watch. "I told the guys I'd meet them at Dakota's," he told her, referring to his band and the club they occasionally played at in town. "Strictly as a favor to the owner. Want to come by later with Shane and Mollie? Maybe we'll even let Mollie sing a set."

Jeannie laughed. Her daughter fancied herself the next singing sensation. "Count on it." She gave him an impulsive hug. "Things *will* work out, Frank. I have a feeling."

He nodded, strictly for Jeannie's sake. He wasn't nearly so sure as she was.

Chapter Twelve

The atmosphere in Dakota's was just what Frank wanted. The lighting was dim and the air hung, thick and melancholy, around the shoulders of the patrons. He sat perched on the stool in the small section that the owner, Jimmy, had set aside as a stage on the Friday nights that he provided entertainment. The band had looked surprised and pleased when he had walked through the door of the pub-style saloon earlier. He'd been reluctant to come at all, until Joe Fraser had all but shamed him into it.

He couldn't go on mooning indefinitely.

Wasn't that what he had said to Donna? That you had to bury the past and move on?

Still, it felt soothing to sit here, amid the shadows, and pretend he was still with her.

The song came to him without any thoughts.

As if he had no choice, the notes for "Greensleeves" seemed to flow from his fingers to the strings of his guitar. Joe, the lanky lead guitarist, exchanged looks with the other three men in the band. That wasn't the opening number they'd agreed upon. With a shrug, he joined in. A moment later, the others followed.

Frank began to sing, his baritone voice swelling with the pain and mournfulness of a love gone by.

Everyone was quiet.

The door at the front of the pub opened and a shaft of light from the street lamp slashed the darkness like a thin stiletto. Frank looked up and saw Jeannie entering, herding Mollie before her. Shane was with them.

Frank missed a chord.

There were three other people with Jeannie.

He had no idea how he got through the song, or the two that followed. He played them all as if he were enmeshed in a dream. And maybe he was. Maybe he was just asleep and had conjured her up in his brain.

It wouldn't be the first time.

"We'll take a short break now, ladies and gentlemen," Frank murmured into the microphone. Very carefully he set his guitar against the stool. "I'll be back in a few minutes." The promise was meant for the men behind him, but he was looking straight ahead.

Like a man who didn't know whether he was asleep or awake, Frank crossed to one of the larger tables in the pub. The table where she sat.

Mollie didn't wait for her uncle to reach them before she began bouncing up and down in her chair. Excitement shone in her wide eyes. "Mommy says you're going to let me sing tonight, Uncle Frank. Are you?"

"Maybe later, Squirt." Even before he answered, Frank was engulfed in hugs and arms that encircled his waist and the lower portion of his chest. Stephen had almost over-turned his chair in his haste to reach him. Warmth flooded Frank even as disbelief held him captive. He laid a hand on each boy's head. "How've you guys been?"

"Awful. We missed you, Frank," Stephen declared.

"Yeah," Taylor verified. "It hasn't been the same without you."

"Well, I certainly missed you." An arm now around each, Frank looked across the table at Donna. Dressed in a two-piece, vanilla suit, she looked wonderful. Better than wonderful. She looked like a dream come to life. But dreams, he reminded himself, weren't real. Frank slowly slipped his arms away. "Hello, Donna," he said almost formally.

The roar of a Conair engine seemed to be vibrating not just in her stomach but all through her. "Hello, Frank."

Her voice, like whiskey and honey on a cold day, poured through his veins. "What brings you to this out-of-the-way place?"

He was going to circle her slowly. All right, she could handle that. "The same thing that brought the boys."

A knowing smile curved about his lips. "Your charter plane."

Didn't he know why she was here? she wondered. Couldn't he see? "In part."

Impatience drummed through Jeannie's veins as she watched and listened to this byplay. They were acting like two opponents at a sideshow, sizing each other up. They needed a little privacy. Barring that, they needed to be in each other's arms.

Jeannie turned toward her husband. "Shane, why don't you feed the jukebox? Maybe Frank and Donna would like to dance."

"Mom doesn't dance anymore," Stephen volunteered. "Not for a long, long time. Almost forever."

Probably since her husband had died, Jeannie guessed. She offered Donna a sympathetic smile. She'd never been widowed, but she knew what it felt like to suddenly find yourself alone with a child to care for.

"Then it's high time she got back to it." Jeannie squeezed the woman's hand as Shane went off to the jukebox in the back. Donna's fingers were icy. Jeannie knew the feeling. "It's like riding a bike and kissing," Jeannie confided to her. "You never really forget how."

Taylor looked impressed. "Can you ride a bike and kiss at the same time?"

Jeannie winked at the boy. "It takes practice, but it can be managed." Music began to float through the air. Something sweet and sentimental. Perfect.

Jeannie smiled, pleased. "Ah, he found it." She looked at her brother expectantly. "Frank, I believe that's your cue."

Frank nodded toward his sister, his eyes on Donna. "She's always been bossy." He extended his hand to Donna. "I'm willing if you are."

Her heart hammered so hard in her throat, she was afraid that it would come out. When it didn't, Donna took his hand and rose. "Yes."

He smiled as he led her to a small area that was cleared off for dancing. It was hardly six feet square, but he wasn't planning on doing a whole lot of moving, he thought as he eased her against him. His body tightened and his emotions flowed, escaping. The faint, heady fragrance she wore seeped into his senses and he thought of springtime and new beginnings.

Say something, stupid, she upbraided herself. She'd just moved heaven and earth to come here, rearranging her life on a wing and a prayer because she'd finally come to her senses. Now here she was, dancing with him and doing an imitation of the Sphinx.

"I didn't know you could sing." It wasn't brilliant, but it was a start.

"There's a lot about me you don't know." He paused, waiting for her to say something. When she didn't, he prodded, "What *are* you doing here?"

Nerves scratched at her with sharp talons. She felt as if she were reaching for the brass ring and suddenly didn't know if her arms were long enough. What if he'd rejected her? He had the right after the way she'd acted.

She stalled for time. "Dancing."

"Besides that." He could feel her heart hammering against him, could feel the slight tremble of her body. It was warm in the room. "All right. Let's start with something easier. How did you find me?"

That she could answer. "You were right. It's not that big a town. I just asked around and someone told me where you live. Jeannie saw me knocking on your door and said that you weren't home." A smile came to her lips. "She guessed who I was. It must have been Taylor and Stephen who gave me away."

"Must have."

Why was he being so stoic? Was she making a fool of herself? Donna pressed on. "She offered to bring me here." She licked her lower lip, running out of courage. "To bring *us* here."

He arched a brow. "All right, now the payoff." The song ended, but another ballad began. Shane must have done a lot of feeding, Frank thought. Frank gauged that he had enough time for one more dance, before he had to get back to the band, so he pressed on. "*Why* are you here?"

She'd been hoping that he would spare her. "Do you have to ask?"

"Yes, I do."

Donna accepted that. "I guess I deserve that." She took a breath, but no words came. Her eyes met his. She couldn't read them, didn't know if she was even welcome anymore. "You're not going to make this easy, are you?"

Dakota's was crowded, even for a Friday night, but all he saw was her. All there was was Donna. Even so, he wasn't going to allow himself to get carried away this time. He was going to be very, very sure before he allowed his fancy to take flight again.

"Should I? As I remember, we didn't part all that amicably."

No, they hadn't. She had lain on her bed, fighting back tears as she had heard her front door close. And then she had spent long, agonizing days trying to get over him, trying to get her life back on an even keel. But there was no even keel anymore. And she had lived by the telephone, hoping that he would call.

"You didn't call."

"No, I didn't." He swayed lazily with the music, trying not to let the brush of her body get to him, trying not to want her again the way he had before. Trying to tell himself that he could resist this time and all the while knowing that it was a lie. "I wanted to, but the next move had to be yours."

She nodded and looked up at him, wanting him to understand what it had taken for her to come here, for her to risk her heart one more time. "I moved."

His fingers tightened a little around hers. "And?"

She took a deep breath. He wanted it all, didn't he? Every *t* crossed, every *i* dotted. "I'm here, checking Wilmington Falls out." She fumbled with her forward pass, feeling vulnerable. "You're right. It is charming."

"Are you making a travelogue for your business, or is there something more permanent in the offing?"

It was frightening to admit, but she had to. There was no other way. She had already leapt over the chasm to his side.

"Permanent. I thought over what you said and you were right." *C'mon, Donna, you've come this far.* Like a highboard diver, she braced herself and then plunged. "Frank, when you left, nothing seemed the same anymore. The boys were still going to school, I was still working. Angelina had returned. Lisa was better than ever. But nothing, *nothing* was the same."

The dim lighting danced along her lips. They glistened as she spoke, making him ache for her. He forced himself to listen.

"It was as if a death had occurred. Another death," she said quietly. "There was no more laughter, no more good feelings. And all the boys did was talk about you. Incessantly."

Frank laughed as he looked over toward the table. Jeannie and Shane appeared to be entertaining all three children. He liked the picture that made. "I do have a way of getting to people."

"Yes, you do. You certainly got to me."

As he held it, he pressed her hand to his chest, absorbing the warmth. "How?" he asked softly. "How did I get to you?"

He definitely wanted it all, she thought. "You want me to say it?"

Just once, he needed to hear it. To hear her tell him that she loved him at least a fraction as much as he did her. "Yes."

Donna looked around. There were people standing alongside the wooden bar and packed in around the tables. The men he played with were onstage, sitting around and chatting over beers. It was a full house. "In front of all these people?"

"Yes. You can use the microphone."

It was meant as a joke. He was surprised when she abruptly stepped back and then walked away from him.

Nice going, Harrigan. Now you did it. He'd managed to scare her off.

Frank hurried after Donna, then stopped as he saw that she wasn't returning to the table. Instead, she was walking toward the impromptu stage.

As he watched in disbelief, she took possession of the microphone. Joe made one attempt to stop her, but Donna waved him back with the authority of a woman who had a mission.

She wasn't good about expressing her feelings. But she couldn't lose him. Not twice. Summoning all her courage, Donna looked out into the sea of faces she didn't know, the sea of faces who would become her neighbors. "I love you, Frank Harrigan. And I was wrong. You were right."

There was approximately one second of silence before hoots, laughter and cheers met her announcement.

Several people around Frank slapped him on the back. Someone pumped his hand and said, "Congratulations. She's a looker all right." He had no idea who said it. All he was aware of was Donna walking back toward him.

Donna tossed her hair as she looked at him. Triumph shone in her eyes. "There, I said it." Her voice softened. "And I mean it."

He was oblivious to the crowd that was steadily gathering around them. "What finally changed your mind?"

"I figured that if I had to deal with the downside of caring about you, I might as well enjoy the upside of it, as well."

"What about the business?" he prodded.

She shook her head, still bemused at the turn of events. "That was the oddest thing. Both my mechanic and my main pilot came to me within hours of each other, saying that they were tired of living in a major city. They wanted to move out to somewhere more peaceful. Somewhere like a little town in northern California." The wording, almost identical, had been positively eerie. A whimsical smile shifted over her lips. "It's as if someone up there wants us to be together."

He touched her face and she felt his love flowing from his fingertips. "Someone down here does, too."

And she was grateful for that, so grateful. "I'm relocating my main office to Riverdale." Donna took a deep breath and plunged ahead. "Now, if that position you offered me two weeks ago is still open, I'd like to fill it."

He looked at her blankly. "What position?"

Had he changed his mind? Courage began to flag as she wondered if she had wantonly sabotaged her own future because she'd been afraid to soar with the eagles. This was an awfully public place to be humiliated. "Wife."

He grinned broadly, unable to maintain a straight face any longer. "It's still open. It was always going to remain open—unless you filled it."

When he took her into his arms and kissed her, Frank was surrounded by a good-size portion of Wilmington Falls's population, as well as Donna's sons and his niece. He didn't notice any of them.

All he was aware of was Donna, and the rainbow he felt spreading within him.

Epilogue

It was time.

It had been a year since her parents-to-be had "found" each other and gotten married. And now it was time.

Erin was fairly jumping up and down on her cloud.

They were going to have a lively time of it—she just knew it. And she was going to have brothers to play with her and sing to her.

A secret smile curved her tiny mouth. Wouldn't Jonathan be surprised when he found out that she was to be his cousin? But Jonathan wouldn't know, wouldn't realize that she had followed his lead and brought her parents together. The sudden urge to see Seattle, the "chance" change in flight assignments, the pregnant woman, Greg's abrupt departure, Rafferty's and Walter's desire to move to the country, all that were machinations she had arranged.

But not the love. Never the love. *That* her parents had delivered on their own.

And soon, like Jonathan, she wouldn't remember any of it. Not consciously.

But Erin had a feeling that, deep down in their souls, they'd know. She and Jonathan would recognize each other and somehow know.

She clapped her hands together and laughed to herself.

She was going to look like her daddy and have long lashes and thick dark hair like her mother. The rest she hadn't decided upon yet, but it didn't matter.

What really mattered had been taken care of. She was getting the parents she wanted. The parents who would make all the difference in the world to her.

"Are you ready?" the Overseer asked, his deep voice rumbling along the surface of the clouds.

She looked up, not seeing him. Not seeing anything except the long, white tunnel that led to earth. And to love.

"Ready!"

The Overseer wasn't completely certain, but he thought he heard a tiny cry of Geronimo! just before the angel disappeared down the tunnel. He shook his head as he drifted away.

Her parents were going to have a handful with that one, he thought.

* * * * *

Dark secrets, dangerous desire...

Lovers DARK AND DANGEROUS

Three spine-tingling tales from the dark side of love.

This October, enter the world of shadowy romance as Silhouette presents the third in their annual tradition of thrilling love stories and chilling story lines. Written by three of Silhouette's top names:

LINDSAY McKENNA
LEE KARR
RACHEL LEE

Haunting a store near you this October.

Take 4 bestselling love stories FREE

Plus get a FREE surprise gift!

Special Limited-time Offer

Mail to Silhouette Reader Service™

3010 Walden Avenue
P.O. Box 1867
Buffalo, N.Y. 14269-1867

YES! Please send me 4 free Silhouette Romance™ novels and my free surprise gift. Then send me 6 brand-new novels every month, which I will receive months before they appear in bookstores. Bill me at the low price of $2.19 each plus 25¢ delivery and applicable sales tax, if any.* That's the complete price and—compared to the cover prices of $2.75 each—quite a bargain! I understand that accepting the books and gift places me under no obligation ever to buy any books. I can always return a shipment and cancel at any time. Even if I never buy another book from Silhouette, the 4 free books and the surprise gift are mine to keep forever.

215 BPA ANRP

Name	(PLEASE PRINT)	
Address	Apt. No.	
City	State	Zip

This offer is limited to one order per household and not valid to present Silhouette Romance™ subscribers. *Terms and prices are subject to change without notice. Sales tax applicable in N.Y.

USROM-94R   ©1990 Harlequin Enterprises Limited

The Loop™

Is the future what it's cracked up to be?

This August, find out how C. J. Clarke copes with being on her own in

GETTING IT TOGETHER: CJ
by Wendy Corsi Staub

Her diet was a flop. Her "beautiful" apartment was cramped. Her "glamour" job consisted of fetching coffee. And her love life was less than zero. But what C.J. didn't know was that things were about to get better....

The ups and downs of modern life continue with

GETTING IT RIGHT: JESSICA
by Carla Cassidy in September

GETTING REAL: CHRISTOPHER
by Kathryn Jensen in October

Get smart. Get into "The Loop!"

Only from

Silhouette®

where passion lives.

Silhouette
SPECIAL EDITION

WILD RIVER

Maddening men...winsome women...and the untamed land
they live in—all add up to love!

A RIVER TO CROSS (SE #910)
Laurie Paige

Sheriff Shane Macklin knew there was more to "town outsider"
Tina Henderson than met the eye. What he saw was a generous
and selfless woman whose true colors held the promise of love....

Don't miss the latest Rogue River tale, A RIVER TO CROSS, available
in September from Silhouette Special Edition!

SEWR-5

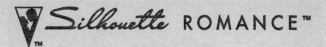

Silhouette ROMANCE™

presents

TIMELY MATRIMONY
by
Kasey Michaels

Suzi Harper found Harry Wilde on a storm-swept beach. But this handsome time traveler from the nineteenth century needed more than a rescuer——he needed a bride to help him survive the modern world. Suzi may have been a willing wife, but could a man from the past be a husband for all time?

Look for *Timely Matrimony* in September, featured in our month of